Alphabet

for

H St

BARBARA O'DONNELL

iUniverse, Inc.
Bloomington

Alphabet for H Street

iUniverse books may be ordered through booksellers or by contacting:

iUniverse
1663 Liberty Drive
Bloomington, IN 47403
www.iuniverse.com
1-800-Authors (1-800-288-4677)

ISBN: 978-1-4502-8476-9 (SC)
ISBN: 978-1-4502-8466-0 (ebook)

Printed in the United States of America

iUniverse rev. date:1/17/11

DEDICATED TO STUART

Thank you to the muse who awakened me to this creative form via which I told this story over 40 years ago and who has helped me work on it ever since. To those friends who read the manuscript through the years and encouraged me to continue working on it. To Kermit Cain, Janine Harrington, and Alan Harrington who typed, advised, edited, and helped me launch the book.

CONTENTS

ALPHABET FOR H STREET

The year? 1969. The setting? A battered duplex apartment on H Street in Sacramento, California. This is the story of Dorie and me, and our friends, and the men in our lives.

1969 was a time of transition. Everything was changing. The messages and role models of our childhoods clashed with the new reality. Dorie and I had been born into rural communities where roles for men and women were fixed. Everybody knew what was expected. The experience of our urban and suburban peers weren't much different. By 1969, Dorie and I were college graduate students who were totally confused about expectations, ours and everybody else's.

We were anomalies, coming from the working class, yet getting college degrees. It was unplanned. It wasn't a hope of our families. After high school, we married and went to work. That was what we were supposed to do. Dorie had a daughter, something else she was expected to do. She was a housewife. I was a part time housewife and worked in a typing pool for a big company. Then, both of our worlds began to crumble, to fall apart, and to change dramatically. Dorie left an abusive husband, and I left a workaholic husband. Suddenly, we were on our own. We had no idea what the new rules were, nor did our girlfriends.

Timidly, I decided to take classes at the community college. And there I fell in love with learning just as I had in elementary school. Reading was my passion. I began to see that I could make a living by reading. I became a literature major and planned to become a teacher. I didn't have to stay in a bad marriage or be a housewife or typist. I had better options with degrees and credentials. And then I met Dorie who was going through the same metamorphosis.

We were eclectic women who could discuss Henry James's literary theme while we baked a cake. We could decipher Blake's poetry while crocheting a scarf. We could contemplate Hemingway's depiction of women while making a bouillabaisse. We flowed from recipes to rhetorical devises with ease. But there was one area of our life where we got stopped cold! And that was our relationships with men. Who could figure the 'crathurs" out? What did they want? Would they call after the first date? With all of our newfound sophistication and progress as intellectually gifted women, there was that part of us that still looked for a prince charming, and he was not to be found.

We met in graduate school at Sacramento State University. Well, actually I had been aware of her for some time because of those green shoes! Sitting in an English class at the community college, I had noticed the woman wearing soft green shoes. She was willowy, with short dark curly hair and snapping brown eyes. She seemed very smart. She talked in class and had coffee with professors after class. I had seen her in the Student Union. I wouldn't have considered saying a word in class. I was frightened to death to reveal how dumb I might be.

My first semester at Sacramento State, I was walking along to class when up ahead of me in the crowd, I spied those green shoes. I felt like I was seeing an old friend even though I didn't know her name. But here she was, someone from my community college past. For the next two years, I occasionally had a class with her, but we never spoke. And then one day in a Hemingway seminar in graduate school, I found myself sitting next to her. A stupid classmate, a retired military officer, was reading his paper about <u>The Sun Also Rises</u>. Finally, I couldn't stand it anymore. His notions were ridiculous. "He's full of shit," I wrote on a notepad and handed it to her in frustration.

"You got that right," she wrote back. "Want to have coffee after class and talk about it?"

So off we went to the Student Union where we began a conversation that has lasted fifty years. At the time, it was spring semester, and I remembered the day we picked up a flier announcing that Dr. Worth was taking a group of students to Ireland and Scotland that summer. The Celtic world. Just imagine such a trip. The more we thought about it, the more determined we were to sign up. We both came from Irish or Scottish immigrant families, and I was working on my master's thesis on Irish mythology and literature. The problem was that neither of us had any money. But that didn't stop us. We plotted and planned, took every part time job we could find, had garage sales, eventually sold our cars. Mid-June found us floundering under the weight of four big suitcases, heading toward the airport where we would meet our group. We were so excited, so filled with anticipation, and we would have had a great summer adventure together if I hadn't run away with an unemployed Irish balladeer my third week at the Kilkenny Seminary.

Dorie covered for me, went on to Scotland with the group, and had her own romantic adventure with Jimmy Braden, an itinerant sheep shearer. Many years later, Dorie and I were on a bus going from Belfast to Donegal discussing the summer trip "that never was and the men that were part of it."

"My God," she said, "a sheep shearer and unemployed balladeer – we certainly set our sights high, didn't we?" We laughed and laughed about it as the bus chugged along the mountain road. We certainly didn't laugh about it at the time. The thing was that I had betrayed the friendship. Here we were coordinating our time and money together to travel all over Ireland and Scotland once the literary course at Kilkenny Seminary was finished, and I left the plan to run off with a man. It never occurred to me that it was a betrayal because from my teenage days on, when a boy came along, girlfriends took second place. Boys came first. That was the undeclared rule. There were so many rules of behavior, roles set in cement, that we never questioned until that incredible year that we shared the rent on H Street. The Celtic trip was over, grad school was about over, and we began to realize that the old mores with which we'd been raised were over. But what new guidelines were there for two divorced, professional women? People in the English Dept. called us the NO NONSENSE GIRLS. We seemed to have our shit together in the language of the day. But we didn't yet know who we were, and who we would become. So we stumbled through jobs, family relationships, girlfriends, dating rituals, and love affairs, talking for hours and hours, trying to figure out our lives.

These are our stories neatly filed in alphabetical order.

CAT

My name is Catherine Winston Fitzgerald. I've been known as Cat forever, and after my tryst with Joe Byrne, I purloined his last name and have kept it ever since. I grew up in rural Iowa on a farm that had been homesteaded by my great grandparents, Irish immigrants. There was an intrigue about being Irish, never defined by my parents, but there all the same. There were no stories handed down, no genealogy done when I was growing up, and no notion about Irish history or why those sturdy souls had immigrated. Yet, there was that intrigue always present. I was told to be proud of being Irish. I never questioned it.

My parents' marriage broke up when I was ten, something unheard of in our small town, and my mother found a new mate and moved with him to Sacramento, CA. Of course in those days, there was no discussion of custody or moving a child. My mother just went to California. That was that. I was supposed to write letters to my father which I did sometimes. It was difficult because I didn't know what to say. Every summer, I was sent to Iowa to live with grandparents on both sides, and my Dad and his new family. It was the July ritual which went on until I graduated from high school. Then it was up to me to make travel plans and pay for it.

My California parents weren't social. In fact, looking back they isolated themselves, living in California, with their faces turned toward Iowa, remembering the good old days, anxious to get those weekly letters from my grandmother and my aunts. My stepfather's side rarely wrote. What were my days like? They mirrored my mother's. We worked from morning to night. We watched TV in the evenings. We went to church, cleaned the house, did the washing and ironing, took care of the two siblings born two and four years after the move. My mother worked as a secretary for the State, my stepfather worked as a carpenter, and I worked as a student and baby sitter. The only break happened in July when I made that long trip by train to Iowa.

We moved quite often, from one suburban house to another. I went to a different school every year until high school when my parents had finally settled down for a few years. And eventually I had the stable enough life style to begin to make friends. I brought them home. My mother hated them. All of them. We had a closed family. There were to be no intruders, and here I was, bringing them into the house. I got the message, but I was a gregarious type like my father and his side of the family, and I kept on making friends, but I didn't talk with them on the phone or invite them over, or go to their houses for visits or sleepovers.

The only friends that my mother didn't dispute, indeed, seemed to encourage, were boys. Boyfriends were just fine. That's as nature intended, and I dated long before I should have, and had no boundaries on where I went or how late I stayed out if I was with a boy. By my sophomore year, my steady boyfriend had a nice car, and my mother seemed proud of it.

I was groomed to get married after exiting high school. I planned a wedding with my steady even though he didn't seem too interested. I had a fantasy in my own head about how everything would look, my dress, the bridesmaids, the cake, the flowers.

I talked about it to my girlfriends, rarely my mother, and rarely to my beau who was more interested in working on his car than listening to my prattle on about matching shoes for the bridesmaids' dresses.

And then in my senior year, all hell broke loose. The beau dumped me for another girl. I had a hope chest filled with embroidered linens collected since I was a freshman. I had a set of stainless steel silverware purchased on the payment plan. I had a dresser scarf, and a set of six matching water glasses. Now what?

Three weeks later, a girlfriend introduced me to a racy, good looking guy from my high school, a member of the swim team. Oh, what a hunk! Within two weeks, the previous beau was forgotten. I went out with Tim. We went to the prom together. We went to the graduation together and the all night grad party. After graduation, I applied and went to work for the State as a typing I. Tim played. Instead of dating, he'd call in the late evening and ask me to sneak out my window, meet him down the road, and then we'd drive to a secluded place to make out. After a few weeks of these escapades, my stepfather nailed the window shut, and said that I shouldn't be dating a "beaner" in the first place. Tim had a Hispanic last name. I didn't know what a beaner was. Finally, I called him, getting up all of my nerve, to try and ferret out of him what was going on, and why we weren't dating. He told me that he wasn't going to see me anymore. He was headed for college, and he wanted to date college "women." I felt ashamed of my status and hung up.

I ran into Tim about five years later. His college career had lasted one semester. He had to drop out to marry his present girlfriend. He was cleaning swimming pools for a living. "Whadaya have going?" he asked.

"I work part-time for the State and I'm a junior at Sacramento State," I said smiling at him.

"Shit," he said, and made excuses to get away from me.

My friends were married. Several dropped out of high school, pregnant, to marry. Some went off to college right out of high school and were married by the end of their sophomore year. My best friend, Diana, had run off with a carney, if you can believe that. She found herself working the fruit picking circuit with him. She had two babies. I kept in touch with her mother. When her youngest child was six months old she came home to her mother, got a decent state job, and we renewed our friendship.

I was stifled at home. I was twenty and desperately wanted to be out on my own. But I had no girlfriend with whom to share the rent, and when it got right down to it, I was scared to strike out on my own. I had been dating Cal for about a year. He was tall, athletic, cute, a hard worker, and inarticulate. But when he put a ring on my finger the Christmas after I started going out with him, I was thrilled.

Then there was the matter of a church wedding. Cal didn't belong to my fundamentalist church and wasn't interested in joining. The church declined to marry a believer with an unbeliever. Plus my parents didn't seem excited about paying for a wedding, and I didn't have much in savings.

Cal took me home to meet his family. They seemed generous and welcoming. I should have known that I had attracted an isolated group just like the family I was leaving, but I didn't pick up on the signs until Cal and I had set a wedding date for the following August. "Oh," his mother said, "we don't believe in public, big weddings." Neither of Cal's older siblings had had such a wedding.

"Don't they want to invite all of their friends to a nice wedding and reception?" I asked Cal.

"What friends?" he quipped.

So we decided to make everybody happy by going to Reno one weekend and getting married by the Justice of the Peace. Why Reno? I have no idea where that idea came from. We weren't twenty-one yet, so we couldn't gamble or order a drink at the casinos. I can't remember what we were thinking.

We settled into an apartment where I felt lonely and miserable. I spent a few days arranging wedding gifts in the cupboards while Cal left early to work construction with his father. I had this terrible feeling that I had done something wrong. But within two weeks I was back to work and classes at American River began. The first night of class when I prepared to go out, Cal had a fit. "I thought once we got married, you'd quit going to school," he said angrily.

"Why would you think that?" I asked, going out the door. We never discussed it further. Within a few months, we bought a small house a few blocks from his parents' home. You could buy a house in those days for $500 down and $120/month. The outside yard looked like a park. The inside was shabby, and I hadn't a clue what to do with it. I didn't do yard work. The only thing that I did know was how to clean. Eventually, I spruced up the house adding little touches here and there, buying and refinishing furniture from the Thrift Shop. I began to understand how to make a nest.

Our lives together took on the quality of roommates. Cal worked late hours, even on weekends. I did my thing with a part-time job and took 18 units a semester to get through Sacramento State. Our only social life was going over to his folks' house on Sunday nights for a barbeque, but even that social life deteriorated when his sister ran off with an abusive boyfriend, exiling herself from the family, and his brother committed suicide after the breakup with his teenaged sweetheart. Cal's mother just fell apart, just went crackers, and his poor Dad tried to hold things together, but our family evenings were over.

Then one day I went to the grocery store and my life changed forever. A young man began bagging my groceries. I looked up at him and felt as if I'd been slammed against the wall. Jamie. His name tag said Jamie. I couldn't breathe. Stunned, I led him to my car and watched him put the groceries into the back seat. He straightened, looked at me intently for a few minutes, smiled, and retreated into the store. I drove home in a haze.

I passed through some invisible threshold leaving reality behind. I floated in wisps of adolescent fantasy. My logical no nonsense psyche froze. I had to see him again.

So, the next day I went back to the store and searched for him. I found him in produce. I stood beside the broccoli staring at him. And he stared back. And then he said he got off work at 4:00, and why didn't I drive by and pick him up? And I did.

We had nothing to say to each other. We made small talk about nothing and drove around aimlessly until I found a secluded place in a park with nobody around. He reached for me, and I reached for him. And that is what we did for three weeks.

The logic began to unthaw. I talked to Dorie. "Why doesn't he ask me out, why don't we drive around in his car, have coffee or a beer or something?"

"Sounds like a married man," she said.

"Huh?" I never considered such a thing.

"Ask him," she said, "he'll run like a rabbit."

I asked, and he did, even transferring to another store.

"He was a married man!" I complained to Dorie.

"Yeah, and you are a married woman," she said gently.

Oh, shit! I was so busy being angry at him, I left my own behavior out of the picture. Now what? The problem was that I had felt something that I hadn't felt for years, about five to be exact. All of my being was invested in working and studying. All emotionality had been driven underground, and now like a volcano it erupted. What was I going to do? Once unrepressed, always unrepressed, and I knew it.

I wanted out of the humdrum trap that I had made for myself, and that could only mean one thing. I had to leave Cal, and begin a life of my own. So in a fit of fantasy and piqué, I packed up and left with no explanation. I left the property, the furniture, the carpets, the art works given by Cal's parents, everything behind. I packed my clothing, old hope chest carefully putting the things I'd come into the marriage back inside it. I packed my good china and silverware, most importantly, my books and typewriter, and I moved out into a furnished apartment in midtown. Cal was surprised, hurt, angry, very angry, and filed for divorce quickly, having his lawyer write into the agreement that I wouldn't indulge in community property. I quick-claimed the property over to Cal. And that was that.

We never talked about our lives, our feelings, what went wrong, nothing. My life with Cal, and his with me, was finished.

So, here I was, 28 years old, divorced, hired in March to teach English at a suburban junior high school after the previous teacher had a heart attack, and working on my master's thesis in Irish mythology and literature. That's when Dorie suggested that we take that summer trip to Ireland and Scotland.

DORIA PATRICIA MCKENZIE

Dorie was smart and brave and an adventurer. I knew that right off the bat. As I said, those green shoes were the key to our friendship. Her story went something like this. She was born and raised in Yakima, Washington. Her parents' marriage ended when she was fourteen, and her father went off to Seattle to work on the docks, and her mother sank into fundamentalism, Christian fundamentalism. Dorie was shocked when her father left, and tried to console her mother, but mother and daughter had always had an antagonistic relationship, and it only got worse.

"It's an old tradition in my family," she said smiling as she told me her story. "Running off with men." It seemed that the girls in the family going back from time immemorial were nice little things, well mannered, pretty, good at school, and then they turned fifteen, and all hell broke loose. "My great grandmother ran off with a traveling salesman and ended up in Yakima, alone with two kids, my grandmother eloped with a farm worker, my mother married my rancher father at fifteen, and I ran off with James at the same age." She sighed thinking of her daughter, Chloe, who had just married at seventeen after spending two years running away and hanging out with one low-life group after another. "I guess it's Chloe's turn now."

Dorie had met James at a drive-in where she worked after school. He was twenty-one, good looking, and seductive. He began taking her out. She could pass for twenty-one, so they drank beer in the Yakima bars and danced the nights away. Dorie was in love. Two days after her sixteenth birthday, they married at City Hall, her mother signing for her because of her age.

James worked construction, many weeks out of town, and when Dorie found herself pregnant, and James gone most of the time, she moved from their apartment back in with her mother. Her daughter was born, and Dorie remembered they day clearly when her mother swept into the bedroom and handed her a breast pump, telling her that if she continued to breast feed, she'd ruin her figure. Grandma always had to run the show.

So, Dorie was very happy when James returned several months later, and said he'd gotten a full-time job on a crew in Sacramento, CA, and they'd be moving. They settled into the suburbs. But life with James wasn't easy. He was restless, and she was bored. He was abusive and controlling, watched everything that she did, questioned her constantly, and doled out money in small amounts like it was manna from heaven. He didn't like her making friends of the other housewives in the neighborhood, and if he came home and found one drinking coffee with Dorie in the kitchen, he'd create a scene.

About the only fun they had was going out on Friday nights, pay day. Dorie would find a neighborhood girl to babysit, and off they'd go to piano bars for drinks and dinner. But Dorie found that after two or three nights of babysitting, the girls would refuse to come back, and she'd have to find a new one. What was wrong? Didn't they pay enough? Finally, she found her nerve and asked the latest girl who refused her offer of a job.

"I don't like being pawed on the way home," she said angrily, hanging up the phone. Pawed? James always took the girls home. Dorie felt cold as ice, but she knew she'd better keep her mouth shut.

Eventually, the piano bar scene wasn't enough for James, and he demanded that they eat a quick supper in a coffee shop and go to a porno theatre where Dorie would sit there enduring these humiliating movies, her head in her hands, and then enduring sex with James into the night. It was neither loving nor nice. She came to hate it. Finally, she refused him and had gotten slapped around for her trouble. He told her she was pitiful, no man would ever want her, she couldn't do anything right, and now she wasn't even good in bed anymore. Dorie smoldered in silence.

Dorie had been sending Chloe off to Grandma's in Yakima for a month every summer since she was six years old. James had always ignored the child, but the summer that Chloe was 12, Dorie caught him looking at Chloe in a new appreciative way. She knew what that meant, and she wouldn't have her child hurt. So, she sent her to Grandma's until she could sort things out.

But one problem with Grandma was that awful religion which Dorie had abandoned as soon as she got out of the house. Grandma's sermons frightened Chloe and Dorie would plead with her mother to stop telling the child about sin, and the blood of the Lamb, and hellfire and damnation. She was ignored.

"That's the summer I took a class at American River," Dorie said. A woman at Chloe's school had bragged to her about her own experience at American River, and Dorie decided to give it a try. She was in love at first class, knowing the joy of learning just as she had experienced it in elementary school.

"That's when I got up the nerve to leave James and go to school full time," she said. "God, he was mad, swore that he'd kill me one day, but then he left the state so that he didn't have to pay child support, and mother and I decided it would be best if Chloe stayed with her for the school year since I was living hand to mouth on financial aid and part-time jobs, typing for grad students. She came down to join me for Christmas and Easter vacation, and seemed like the old Chloe, the sparkling, delightful girl, I'd always known. We talked about Grandma's fundamentalism, but now at 13, she was learning to tune it out, or so she said.

School began again, and she went back to Grandma's. I moved about every six months, a cheap place in the suburbs, then my car blew up, and I moved downtown to be near a bus line, and then I moved again and again, always looking for a better place or cheaper rent. And before you knew it, Chloe's 15th birthday came, and the family pattern returned to haunt mother and me.

Chloe began to run away. First from Grandma to me, and then the reverse. She couldn't get settled, refused to go to school, and began hanging out in Yakima and Sacramento with low-lifes, pot smokers, drop-outs. If there was a bottom-feeder within five miles, Chloe would hook up with him or her. Grandma finally put her in a church boot camp, but she ended up on my doorstep after several months. And she'd arrive with the clothes on her back. Nothing more. We'd go to Goodwill and I'd buy her some jeans and T-shirts, her uniform now, a pair of shoes, go on to Penney's for decent underwear, and just try to get her to settle in when she'd either bring all those awful friends over once too often and we'd have a big fight, or she'd skedaddle back to Grandma's. It was driving me nuts.

Today I would have insisted on counseling. Indeed, my counselor at A.R. had advised it, but Chloe wouldn't go, and I was too dumb to push the issue.

Then when she was 17, Grandma did what all the women in my family did. She encouraged Chloe to get married, ran her past a preacher's son who wasn't much good, got her married, he got her pregnant, and that's all there is to that story. She got religion just like mother, is so antagonistic when I try to talk to her on the phone, as if everything is my fault, that I keep my distance.

Guilty. God, I feel guilty. But if there is one thing that I've figured out, it is that there are times when it's either them or you! And by God, it wasn't going to be me. Sometimes I think about that sweet little child that Chloe was. I wonder if she had a decent Dad, if things would have been different. But they are what they are, and there's no going back. I know that I was so distracted with my new life, my studies, my survival, my rogues gallery of beaus and trying to figure out what they were all about that it might seem to Chloe that I abandoned her.

Should I have quit school, gotten a job, and taken care of Chloe was if she was still six? She wouldn't have cooperated in the least. What could have made it better? I don't know. I only know that there is a family pattern so damn deep in our psyches even though we don't really know it or own it that we can't escape it. Me, my sisters, my mother, my grannies back as far as we have stories. It's always this way."

KATE AND JUNE

When I arrived at the H Street duplex in July with Joe Byrne in tow, there was a for rent sign on the opposite flat which faced 37th Street. A rental agent came and went, showing the flat to a few people, but it wasn't until September, Labor Day to be exact, that the new occupants moved in. Kate and June were quite the pair.

I described them as a Shetland and a Clydesdale. Kate was five foot ten inches tall, big boned, plain faced, a commanding figure of a woman. June was petite, couldn't have weighed a hundred pounds, and was curvy and dark. Kate was Irish. June was Italian. Kate worked at a biology lab for the State examining bugs for the Forestry Department. June worked as a clerk and window dresser at Francine's Dress Shop at the Arden Town Mall. Kate wore jeans and T-shirts, June wore fluffy things, capris with matching frilly tops or lacy, poofy, girly dresses. They were about as opposite as two women could be, but they had been best friends since jr. high, and had lived together since graduating from high school in suburban Sacramento. Kate drove a Chevy pickup truck, and June drove a Volkswagen. Dorie and I greeted them when they pulled up in a U-Haul truck and began unloading their things.

We helped them move in, offered them coffee and sandwiches, and gossiped about the landlord and neighborhood. They seemed likeable, pleasant, and June was given to funny quips which we all laughed at. They were interested that we were divorced. Neither of them had been married. June had been engaged once, but had broken it off.

"Pleasant women," I said after they left.

"It's kinda funny to see them together. One is big and strong, the other little and cute. BS and LC." We giggled at the new code words for these neighbors.

"Seems they'll be nice neighbors," Dorie agreed. And so they were.

𝒜

AUGUSTINE

A is for Augustine, the beautiful Mexican architect that Dorie met while working a part time job for the Old Sacramento Foundation. His firm in Mexico had sent him to Sacramento to study how the redevelopment of the waterfront and the old town was being done. I only met him once, but was extremely impressed with his good looks, soft spoken voice, and old world charm and manners. He was angular and muscular and clay colored. And it was love at first sight between the two of them.

They were devoted to each other. They had this otherworldly mystical connection juxtaposed with a lustful, "I can't keep my hands off you" physical connection. They spent dreamy evenings sitting on the front porch steps eating half cantaloupes filled with coffee flavored ice cream. Their love affair was ardent to the extreme, and everything would have been just perfect if Augustine hadn't flown home to Guadalajara and his hidden Mexican wife and five children!

Upon learning that he wasn't coming back as he had promised, and that he had a family in Mexico from one of his colleagues, Dorie went into a deep, heart broken depression. That's where I come in. We had that coffee date at the Student Union, and it wasn't long before we began sharing the intimate stories of our lives, and the first story that Dorie shared was about Augustine. I wanted to fly down to Guadalajara, find the son-of-a-bitch and kill him. I had justified outrage. Dorie had the deepest kind of sadness. All of this happened the spring prior to our Celtic trip. Little did I know that I'd be having a similar experience very soon.

B

BREAK-IN, BYRNE, BUDDIES, AND BANANA SLUG BOB

B stands for Break-In, Byrne, buddies, and Banana Slug Bob. My adventure with Joe Byrne had begun in Ireland some weeks before. Some people send home souvenirs or post cards. I had dragged home a man. Of course, I had no idea what on earth to do with him once I got him. But we had to be together. Sheer determination had gotten us this far. I figured it would keep us going further I would move the earth for Joe Byrne.

While I tried to work out the details, Joe drank everything in sight. He wasn't meant for the 20th century. He was meant for the 12th where he could spend his time fighting with his mates, hunting in the forests, wandering from village to village enchanting the girls with his guitar and ballads. But since he was living in the 20th century and had a wife and two kids, he was supposed to get a job, support his family, enjoy an occasional pint, and contribute to society.

He found it much easier to elope with an American tourist! "Always wanted to see California," he was heard to say as he boarded the big, silver jet. But life in California was quite like Ireland in many ways. Yes, there were freeways with eight lanes of traffic, and everybody seemed to own a car. There were bars where women actually took off their clothes and danced about. He was horrified by this. But after discussing these natural wonders with the locals, they too expected you to get a job and contribute something to the world, like paying for starters. "People just didn't understand the nature of a man," he mused over his breakfast beer. Men were made to slay dragons, entice women and dream dreams. They were made to sing songs, rival each other's strengths, and get drunk. Well, he couldn't find any dragons or rivals, and this new American woman expected him to fit into the modern world. He couldn't sing any songs without his guitar. He had smashed it in a rage after an argument with the American his second evening in Sacramento. What was left? Dreams? Beer? The only sensible thing for an Irishman to do when he finds himself 8,000 miles away from home was to get drunk and stay that way. So, he did.

But I get ahead of myself. We arrived in Sacramento with no money, my household things in storage, and nowhere to stay, except Dorie had had told me the rent was paid on H Street for the rest of the summer, and key to the front door was under the flower pot on the front porch. So, we took a bus from the airport to H Street.

We found no key under the flower pot. Now, how to get into the place? I was exhausted. All I wanted was to slip into oblivion in a clean bed. Joe began trying to open the windows, but none of them would budge. Finally, he climbed up onto the roof from the low hanging front porch latticework, and found a second story window that wasn't locked. He worked his way inside and found a light switch just as the cops arrived and demanded to know why we were breaking into the house. Some neighbor watching our antics had called them.

Joe had come down the stairs, opened the front door, only to be met by two officers, which scared the bejasus out of him. He stood in the doorway with his hands up just like a criminal in the movies.

"Well, officer," I tried to explain, "We're not breaking in, well not really. You see, we just got back from the airport and are supposed to use my friend's apartment until she gets back next month. The key was supposed to be under the geraniums, but we can't find it, so we tried the windows, and himself, there, found one open on the second floor.

"Where have you been?" the officer asked.

"Ireland," I said.

Joe reached into his pants pocket with one hand and drew out his passport, which he waved at the officer who took it and studied its contents.

"And what is this friend's name?" the officer asked.

"Dorie McKenzie," I said.

"Let's go inside," he said. Joe stepped back and we entered the apartment.

"Buddy, put your hands down," one officer told Joe. Joe shoved his hands in his pockets.

"Here," I said taking mail off of the dining room table where Dorie's friend had put it.

"Here's the PG&E bill with her name on it. See? Dorie McKenzie." The policeman took the envelope and studied it. Then he looked to the front porch where our suitcases still stood.

"O.K. folks," he said. "Sounds like your story makes sense. We don't want any more phone calls about you, do you hear?"

"Oh yes," I said as they turned to leave.

"Well, that was some home coning," I said to Joe who slumped into a chair.

"I need a beer," he said.

By now my adrenalin was shooting sparks. All thoughts of a clean bed were forgotten. "I'm calling Diana," I told Joe, "and asking her to bring a six pack. Let's have a homecoming party!"

Diana was my best friend from high school. I gave her a call and a request, and thirty minutes later there she was pulling up to the curb in an old silver Thunderbird. Her crazy brother, Steve, sat beside her. She opened the door to get out tugging on a 12 Pack. The passenger door wouldn't open for some reason, and I saw Steve wearing only red swimming trunks slither through the window and land on his backside on the street. He got up unhurt and retrieved a black stovepipe hat from inside the car and put it on his head. Diana looked glamorous wearing a gold lame pant suit and a long blonde wig. What a pair they were walking up the steps. Joe just stared at them.

"Diana," I yelped at her and headed toward her for a hug. Steve just stood there grinning.

"Got a smoke?" he asked before I began introductions.

"This is Joe, the guy I wrote to you about," I told them. Joe shook their hands.

"Hey, he smells like vanilla cake," Diana volunteered, looking him over. We cracked open some beers and headed toward the couch.

"Nobody got smokes?" Steve asked again.

"No, guess not," I told him. He kept looking around as if a pack would appear out of this air.

"How are you?" I asked my friend.

"In love," she said dreamily. "Been going to church again, and I went up to the altar the other night to get rid of my sins, and I was praying so loud, and then I looked up and saw him."

"God?" I asked.

"No, Ron Rasmussen," she chortled. "He's the new youth minister, and I just know we are meant for each other.

God's going to see to it this time." I thought about her failed marriage to a carnie, her odd love affairs with misfits, her strange family.

"Well, what's this Rasmussen fella have to say," I asked.

"Oh, we haven't talked or anything," she said. "He's married, right now, but I know by the way he looks at me that we'll be together."

"He's a priest kind of thing?" Joe asked. She nodded and he murmured something about American women, something I didn't quite catch. Steve was asking for cigarettes again, and then headed for the door.

"Don't go far," Diana called to him, unconcerned. We continued to chat and Joe continued to drink one beer after another. As I told her about the police incident, he began a tirade about the Garda and a man's home being his castle, and what on earth did those to be fellas want anyway?

"This isn't our home or castle, "I reminded him. "They thought we were breaking in."

About this time, Diana stepped out onto the porch to look for her brother. He had gone up and down the street in his strange get up, knocking on people's doors asking if they had a smoke. We could see him standing on a front porch a few houses down.

"Idiot," she said. "He's an idiot."

About this time, Steve came ambling back up the street just as the police arrived again. They didn't look happy at all to be back. "What's going on?" one yelled at us. Joe stuck his head out of the door, saw who it was, and ran up the stairs. "Some loon from this place is knocking on people's doors asking for cigarettes?" Just then Steve arrived and the police gave him the evil eye.

"Got a cigarette?" he asked the cops. One office fished in his pocket and handed him one.

"Now stop bothering the neighbors," he told Steve. Then he turned to me. "I told you we didn't want anymore trouble from this address," he said.

"Well, you see my friends came over and we were having a few beers, and then this guy disappeared, and we didn't know what he was doing, and they're just about ready to leave, and..."

He interrupted me. "One more call about this address, and I'm running you in. Get your act together. O.K?"

"Yes. Yes," I said. Steve sat on the front step smoking, and Diana finished her beer. "Better be going," she said. "Don't want to end up in jail, but that second officer was really cute, wasn't he?"

I shrugged, she laughed and grabbed Steve by the arm and began steering him toward the car. "Call you tomorrow," she said as she and Steve clamored into the car and pulled off into the night.

"On my God," I said as Joe came back down the stairs.

"Are they all gone?" he asked. "And did they leave any beer?"

It was a bad beginning that only got worse. Joe got angry and smashed his guitar. Joe got angry and took off walking out into the night and didn't come home until daybreak. Joe got angry and took up with a floozy at the 24th Street bar. Joe got angry and blamed me for taking him away from home. Joe got angry after being denied a work permit, and Joe got angry and broke down one night, sobbing as if his heart would break. He wanted to go home. So, I packed his bags, bought him an airline ticket, and borrowed Diana's car to take him to the airport. He was stone cold sober when he got on the plane.

And I was stone cold sober with a terrible ache in my heart. I couldn't cry. I just hurt all over, and the happiest day of the summer came when Dorie came home. We didn't talk about betrayal. We talked about Augustine and Joe and where fiery love affairs got us. Jimmy Braden wrote to say he wanted to come to California. Would she buy him a ticket? And Joe Byrne wrote saying that he had made a terrible mistake by coming home. Those Irish lads had about done us both in in different ways. Dorie had been clear with Jimmy Braden that their summer romance would come to an end in August. It had been a nice interlude in her life. I had been awash in adolescent delusions about Joe Byrne. And what were we going to do about it? The day after Labor Day, the school term began, and we threw ourselves into our work. That was the medicine we needed.

October loomed. I had just gotten into my school rhythm when in late September I began getting long letters from Joe declaring his undying love and begging me for an airline ticket. He said "he couldn't stick it out in Kilkenny." Everyone hated him for running off with an American even if his cronies were eager to hear him recount his adventures over and over again. His wife disowned him, his mother said she could hardly even go to Mass of a morning, his sister lectured him, his brother smirked, and no one in town would give him a job.

"Hm," I wondered, "What's new? They wouldn't give you a job before I got to Kilkenny. So don't blame that on our love affair."

"What are you going to do?" Dorie asked. I didn't have a clue. At the onset of the first two letters, I felt indignant. After his display of anger when he was in Sacramento, did he really think that I'd bail him out of his society again and bring him back? Bring him back to do what? I worked. He couldn't. How was he going to spend his days? I wrote my concerns which were unanswered. Every few days, a new letter came telling me how much he missed me, couldn't live without me, and to please, please, please send an airline ticket. Basically, he wore me down. I wanted to be with this fiery beautiful man. It was so easy to suspend whatever common sense that I had, to move into fantasy again, and eventually, I bought him a ticket.

Now what? Obviously, I'd have to move. Dorie wasn't about to let Joe move into her flat. But I had promised her I would share the rent. We didn't talk about it. She felt angry and betrayed once again, and I felt guilty. But we didn't talk about it. WE DIDN'T TALK ABOUT IT. She said she'd make do, and I rented a flat some blocks away on 25th Street.

The day Joe arrived at the airport, I was beside myself with nerves. As I waited for him to come down the ramp, I felt like I was going to fall apart, but one glance at him and my heart just raced with anticipation. We rushed into each other's arms. We cried. And we hugged again. And then slowly we made our way to the baggage carousel. All of a sudden, I felt shy as if I had nothing to say to this man, as if I couldn't let on how I felt. And he must have sensed the mood, because he seemed tongue-tied too. His suitcase came, and we made our way to the car, found our way out of the airport, and headed to 25th Street. We were really quiet.

We entered the new flat, and I showed Joe around. He said the place looked grand, just grand. We sat on the love seat, holding hands. "Do you want to unpack?" I finally asked. Yeah, he said. There wasn't much in the suitcase.

God I had to get out of that flat. "Want a beer?" I asked. Of course, he wanted a beer. We walked a few blocks to a neighborhood bar, and went inside. We found a place at the end of the bar, ordered a draft, and slowly he began to talk, telling me all about his travails at home. "They hate me at home," he said, "but they just can't stop talking about it. Jean is in a rage, and won't let me hardly see the kids at all. I wait until she's got them in the pram doing the shopping and then I tail her. She won't have a loud fight on the street."

"But where are you staying?" I asked.

"At the mother's," he said, "and listening to her preach to me day and night, crying about how I used to be such a good boy and where had everything gone wrong. It was the drink. That was all she could think of… the drink. Of course, I collected the dole, but after I gave the mother a few shillings, and Jean when I saw her with the pram, there wasn't much left over to spend in the pubs on the beer and the fags. I had to do some things to get the money, you know."

"Like what?" I asked.

"Ah, never you mind," he said, looking away.

His face was very white, there were dark circles under his magnificent deep brown eyes, and his hair, that jet black hair, curled around his ears and fell into his face. He swept it back with one hand while he talked. He half frowned as he talked, and he drank one beer after another until my money ran out, and it was time to go home. And then we felt awkward again, very awkward. Instead of leaping into bed for a tryst, neither of us quite knew what to do. We shyly took our clothes off. I put on a nightgown in the bathroom, and he left his T-shirt and underwear on. We got into bed and laid there feeling uncomfortable. Eventually, he turned away and so did I, and we went to sleep. I had to get up at 6:00 and get ready for work. Joe was still asleep when I left the house leaving him a note telling him when I'd be home and leaving him a fiver. Something felt like a trap.

I hurried through my day and made my way home feeling very anxious. But there Joe sat watching TV when I came through the door. "Ah, pet, I thought you'd never be home," he said, taking me into his arms and steering me toward the bedroom where we stayed for a long, long time.

Eventually I made us bacon and eggs and toast, the basic meal Joe loved. We watched TV, shared a 6 pack I had brought home, and fell into bed and went to sleep, sated and happy. The next day I got up, went through my day, and rushed home as before, but this time Joe was not in the flat. My heart sank. I waited and waited for the phone to ring or to hear him come up the stairs to the flat's door. At 11:00, I fell asleep only to awaken at 3:00 a.m. when he stumbled into the flat obviously drunk as a Lord and not careful about what he fell over or pushed aside. I pretended to be asleep. This was what happened on Wednesday, Thursday, and Friday. On Saturday, when Joe awoke he seemed surprised to see me. "I don't work on the weekends," I said drolly. "It's Saturday."

"Ah, yeah," he said pouring himself some coffee.

"Joe, what's going on?" I asked calmly. "You're up to your old tricks, going off to that 24th Street bar, probably staying out until the middle of the night. You know this didn't work before and it won't work now. I know that you can't work legally, but with your musical ability, you could get gigs all over town and get under the table money. We could figure out something together until we could get you the right visa or whatever you need. But this isn't Kilkenny where a guy can live off the dole and somehow your family gets supported. You can't live a life watching TV and drinking beer at the 24th Street Bar while I pay the bills."

"You don't understand, pet," he said. "I know all that, but I had to get out of the country and you were my only way out."

"What do you mean you had to get out of the country? Are you talking about Jean and your mother and the fact that nobody in Kilkenny will hire you for anything?"

"Not exactly," he said.

"Well, what exactly?" a strain coming into my voice.

"I can't talk about it," he said, looking across my right shoulder to the wall. "Let's just say that I had to make money somehow in Ireland, and I found a way, but the fucken authorities didn't like my game. I had to get out of the country before they arrested me."

"Arrested you for what? Drugs?"

"No not drugs. Guns," he said, looking right straight ahead at me.

"Guns?" I said in a small voice.

"Yeah, you ever heard of the troubles up North? The IRA? Well, they need guns, see, and they need people in the South to meet the boats that come in to various coves, and to get the so-called cargo to them, you know? They pay well. But I was being watched, see? And I knew it was only a matter of time before the garda would be knocking on me mother's door. I had to get out."

"They paid well, Hm," I said. "So what happened to the money? Why did I have to buy an airline ticket?"

"I gave most of it to the mother, of course," he said.

"Did she question where it came from?" I asked.

He smiled at me as if I was really stupid. "You don't understand, do ya pet?" he said. "You've never been poor. If you are, and you get a windfall, you don't ask questions."

We sat silently for awhile, both smoked a cigarette, thinking.

"Where else can you go?" I asked. "You know staying here isn't the answer. Things will blow up, blow up really badly. In a way they already have, and you've only been here a week."

"You know that I love you more than life," he said softly.

"I do know that, strangely enough, I said. "But it isn't enough, is it?"

"No," he said flatly.

"Let's go for a walk," I suggested, "let's walk over to St. Francis and say a few prayers."

It was a beautiful, late October day with the leaves turning colors, the grasses already dried up and beginning their winter sleep. As we walked home from the church, Joe spoke of England. Liverpool. That might be a place to get lost for awhile. He had a contact there. I filed that information. I fixed a little dinner, sandwiches and salad, and then Joe began pacing, restless, eager for the bar life, and all of a sudden, I didn't care. I handed him a $10 bill, and he left. I cleaned up the kitchen, took a long, hot bath, thinking, thinking, thinking, and eventually cuddled down in bed and went to sleep.

I was awakened about midnight by Joe stumbling into the flat. He came into the bedroom where I sat up in bed and began raving about the superior American, always telling him what to do, always right about everything. The fucking superior American, and then he rushed at me, grabbed my hair and swung his fist front and center into my face. Blood spurted everywhere. We both looked at each other in shock, me because he hit me, and he because he didn't know it was coming.

He sat on the side of the bed and began to cry, and I went into the bathroom to wash my face and put a cold, wet towel to my face. I was frightened, angry, cagey as a cat. I locked the bathroom door and sat on the edge of the tub, listening for any tell tale noise. When the sobbing stopped, I held steady for awhile, and then cautiously opened the door a crack. Joe snored on the bed. I silently put on my jeans and sweatshirt, tiptoed out of the room grabbing my purse and shoes, and left the flat, heading for Dorie's.

I got to Dorie's, used my key to enter, and sat down in the rocking chair and began to cry. I heard her light being switched on in her bedroom, so I called softly to her so that she wouldn't think she was being burglarized. She came down the stairs swiftly and turned on the lamp nearby the rocker. "Jesus Christ," she exclaimed. "What happened to you?"

"He hit me," was all that I could get out. She went into the kitchen, rattled the ice trays, and came back into the room with a tea towel ice pack.

"Hold this up to your face," she said handing it to me gently. I took a Kleenex from its box on the coffee table and patted at my nose and bleeding upper lip before applying the ice.

"Now," she said, "what do you mean he hit you?"

"I don't know. It came out of the blue. He'd been to the 24th Street Bar, as usual, he was drunk, and he began yelling at me for being the superior American, and then out of nowhere, he threw this punch. It shocked us both, blood was everywhere, and then he sat down on the bed and began to cry. I locked myself in the bathroom until I knew he was asleep. And then I hightailed it over here. I don't know what to do."

"Oh yes you do," she said in a stony voice. "My God, he's only been here barely two weeks. I knew this wasn't a good idea."

"He told me why he came," I said, telling Dorie about our conversation of the afternoon. I also unloaded about his every move from the time I picked him up at the airport, the boredom, going back to the 24th Street Bar to hang out with his cronies and the barflies. "Why do I have to love him?" I cried into the towel, "and why does he have to love me? Why did we have to meet up last summer in Ireland, anyway."

"Love," she said sadly. "What on earth does that word mean? You had a fiery, grand adventure, but does love betray you? Smash you in the face? Use your goodwill to provide a hide-away, if his story is true?"

"He could make something of himself," I said softly. "With his looks and voice and guitar, he could make something of himself."

"He already has," Dorie said in a comforting voice. "He is an arrested adolescent, a rebel without a cause, an alcoholic… oh yes, he's a charmer, he's beautiful, but he's a user and an abuser. Send him home for good."

We sat there in the lamplight for awhile, neither of us saying anything. Dorie lit a cigarette, and I rocked in the chair.

"Liverpool," I said, "that's where I'm sending him. I'll get on the phone in the morning and get him a ticket. Dorie nodded, handed me the afghan with which to roll up with on the couch, and slowly made her way upstairs after turning out the lamp light.

The next morning, I called in sick. My face was swollen, and one of my eyes was black. Then I called the airline and booked a one-way ticket to Liverpool from San Francisco, beginning destination, Sacramento. Then I drove home to pack his things. Carefully, I entered the flat only to find him gone out. I locked the doors behind me using the big bolt lock to which he didn't have a key, found his suitcase, and carefully packed his things. I set the case out on the front porch, made myself a pot of coffee, and waited. About noon, Joe appeared with a buzz on. He tried his key but couldn't get through the deadbolt lock. I slowly opened the door, but stood in the doorway. He looked from my battered face to the suitcase. "Jasus, I'm sorry," he said. "I really am, pet."

"I know," is all I could get out. The bravado was gone, the boyish charm, and all I could see in his eyes was concern and guilt. "I bought you a ticket to Liverpool," I told him. "It leaves from Sacramento tomorrow morning at 10:00. Can you get a ride to the airport from one of your friends at the 24th Street Bar?

"Sure," he said in a tiny voice looking down at his shoes. "I have to say good-bye now," I said. "I have to say good-bye. Don't miss that flight." I quietly shut the door, turning all the locks. Joe sat down on one of the steps and put his head in his hands. I sat down on the love seat where I could see him from the window. There we sat for almost an hour. A man on one side of the door, a woman on the other, yet 8,000 miles apart.

Eventually, he stood up, picked up the suitcase and walked down the street. I pulled the linens from the bed and bundled them up with laundry and towels. I straightened the kitchen, washing the coffee pot, and made a call to my landlady to tell her that I would be moving on. By the end of the week, I was firmly ensconced back at Dorie's. And we were back into our habit of talking long into the night about what love between a man and a woman really meant when all was said and done.

BANANA SLUG BOB CASTRO

Banana Slug Bob was the man who came to dinner and wouldn't leave. We had a strict rule on H Street – no overnight guests, and we both stuck to it. We wanted our privacy, and we wouldn't tolerate intruders. If Dorie was asking a friend to come by, she discussed it with me first. And visa versa.

Dorie had dated this grocery store clerk for several weeks when we agreed that we'd invite him to have dinner with us. He came complete with a paper bag holding a 12 pack of beer. On this particular boozy night (his, not ours), he oozed over to the couch after dinner, sat down, and just wouldn't leave. We yawned, we talked about it being "an early day tomorrow," and eventually, I went to bed. He just sat there watching the news on TV, and then the late show with Johnny Carson, opening can after can of beer until eventually, he passed out. Dorie went to bed.

Early the next morning as we emerged from our rooms, she cautioned me that he was probably still on the couch. We peered over the upstairs railing, and sure enough, there he lay, snoring on our couch. "Reminds me of a banana slug," I said, and we both cracked up.

"What am I going to do with him?" Dorie asked.

"Throw the bum out," I said.

"Boy, I couldn't see this coming," Dorie said. "I mean he was light hearted and fun. God damn it!"

Dorie went down the stairs and shook the slug. He wouldn't wake up. She yelled at him. He appeared deaf. She eventually grabbed him by the arm and rolled him off the couch and onto the floor.

"Lemme sleep," he said drowsily.

What to do? Stupidly, we left him alone and got ready for work. We actually left the house with him in it! When we arrived home after work, we found him still on the couch watching TV and drinking more beer. Dorie tried to reason with him.

"Bob, you can't stay here. You have to go home," she said.

"Why, baby?" he reasoned. "You got a good set-up here. You cook, I eat, watch a little TV, drink a little beer…what's the harm?"

"The harm?" Dorie said in a deadly tone of anger. "The harm is that you are in my house. I don't want you here. I don't want you watching TV or drinking beer in my living room. And if you think that I'm interested in cooking for you, you're nuts! Now, get out! What about your apartment? What about your job?"

"Got fired two weeks ago. Gave up my apartment. Got all my stuff in my car."

"Leave or I call the cops," she leveled at him.

"So, call 'em," he said, continuing to stare at the TV.

Dorie looked over at me. I shrugged and went to the phone. Twenty minutes later, two officers knocked on the door looking slightly annoyed. They didn't like domestic calls.

"What's the big trouble?" one of them asked.

"This man," Dorie began. "This man came to dinner last night and won't leave." It sounded so foolish. It was embarrassing to have to say it.

"When did you say he entered the house?" the other office asked.

"Last night," Ann went on. "He stayed the night, and he won't leave," she said, and the cops looked at each other in a knowing way.

"No, you don't understand," she said, reading their thoughts.

"We've dated for a few weeks – he got drunk and slept on the couch. He says he gave up his apartment and lost his job, and won't leave."

"Haven't we been here before," one of the officers said, looking at me with recognition. "Wasn't there some problem with breaking in, a bunch of nuts standing around on the front porch, some guy from Ireland waving his passport?"

"Well, yes I had a problem last summer, but this is another matter. My friend's date won't leave."

The officer nodded his head and rolled his eyes at his partner. He moved to the couch. "Look buddy, what's the problem here?"

Banana Slug Bob knew the jig was up. He flicked off the TV, picked up his bag of beer, and walked right out of the door. The cops followed. And we followed behind them. The four of us watched Banana Slug Bob get into his old Chevy, start it up, and lurch away from the curb.

"Problem seems to be solved, ladies," the officer said.

They smiled and retreated to their car.

"Well, that takes care of that," I said

"How do we get into these situations?" Dorie asked.

"I don't know, but it seems that it could only happen to us," I answered.

Big and Strong and Little and Cute came by after the police left wondering what was going on. They'd seen the police car parked in front of the house. Briefly, we told them the story. Neither woman could believe it. "I met a man like that," LC said. "I met him at the Mall, and we went out for burgers. I liked him. He was about thirty, good looking in a geek kind of way. I mean he looked smart and dressed like a business guy. But after that first burger date, he just kind of hung around, asking me if I had any money. He wanted to go for coffee, or he wanted to get an ice cream cone. At first, I bought. But after a few weeks, I was sick of it, and told him I hadn't any pocket money.

'Well, do you have a credit card?' he asked. Can you imagine the nerve? I told him that I didn't want to see him again. But he persisted, hanging around the store. Then I got to thinking. Why was he always hanging around the store? Didn't he work? I ignored him, but it wasn't long before he began sweet talking my co-worker, and she fell for his line. The same thing happened. Burger date, and then asking her to pay for treats. Then one day, she asked if she could talk to me about the guy, Dave was his name. She said that after two weeks of sharing treats and having long phone conversations, he wanted to move in with her. She had a girlfriend with whom she shared an apartment and didn't know how he'd fit in.

Why do you want him to fit in? I asked her.

'Well, I kinda feel like someone should take care of him,' she answered. 'He doesn't have a job right now, but he's looking for one. He's divorced and has a couple of kids, and his wife is on his back for child support. I just feel sorry for the guy.'

How hard could he be looking for a job when he hung out at the Mall all the time? I mean, it was disgusting. He wasn't looking for a job. He was looking for a woman to take care of him, a Momma. I told her so, but she kept saying that she thought she was in love.

Well, evidently, he moved in, and the girlfriend moved out. Now, my co-worker had to handle the expenses all alone, and she couldn't make it. She was evicted. Now the two of them had nowhere to go, she got madder and madder as she had to sleep in her car for a couple of nights. They had a big fight, and she went home to her parents to get her act together. And you know what? About a month later, we saw him hanging around the Big Beautiful Woman store with that same hangdog appearance. I just knew he was stalking another woman. What a deal. But women fall for it all the time."

BS nodded thoughtfully. "You have to be careful," she said. We all sipped the coffee that Dorie had poured and continued talking about men who used women, just used them up.

C

CAROLYN, CLAUDE, CHLOE, COUNSELORS, AND CAROUSAL SEX

In September we settled into a new school year. I was teaching at a Junior High School in the suburbs, and Dorie was teaching part time in the English Department at Sacramento State University. I was new to teaching and had no idea what to do. I had two hundred fifteen students a day, but no curriculum guide and no books. We were supposed to be creative. Help came from a teacher across the hall named Carolyn. She was organized, bright, and knew just what to do with those kids, most of who didn't give a rat's ass about getting an education.

On my free period, I would sit in the back of her classroom and take notes. She was a wonder. But one day, she came to school wearing dark glassed to hide a black eye. At lunch, she confided in me that her husband of ten years had hit her, and it wasn't the first time. A month later, she said she was leaving him, moving out with her two small children.

She was truly a lost soul. I invited her to dinner, but Dorie didn't like her at all. "She's trouble," Dorie said. And she was absolutely right.

It all began when Evor Price invited me to a party at his apartment. Dr. Price was an elegant man, an English professor at Sacramento State. Dr. Simon North had introduced us. I'd never taken a class from him. He was funny, and had a quick wit. He knew English literature backwards and forwards, and we found that we had lots to talk about. He was twenty years older than me, divorced with two college age sons. The boys lived with their mother, but he saw them on weekends. He was a very social type, but made it quite clear that he didn't want to get "involved," as he said. Dates were strictly for fun. Our first had been on New Year's Eve. We should make no demands on each other, and that was fine by me.

So, he sent me an invitation to his party in late March, a party, he stressed, which was for singles only. I asked him if I could bring Carolyn along, and he said the more the merrier. I thought it would do her good to get out. But the next week, she almost drove me nuts trying to decide what to wear, and how to do her hair.

"We're just going to a party at Dr. Price's apartment," I told her. "It's no big deal."

"Well, what if I should meet someone that I really like?" she asked. "I mean it could happen. I could meet the man of my dreams, and there I'd be wearing my old green skirt."

Yes, our identity was all tied up with having a man in our lives. She'd only left one a month before, and already she romanticized about finding a new one. She did what most of us did. She went from thirty back to sixteen, hoping that some good-looking guy would pay attention to her. So, all that week she fretted about what she should wear to the party.

The night of the party arrived, and Carolyn and I drove out to the suburbs to Dr. Price's apartment. I introduced Carolyn to about a dozen people standing around with drinks in their hands, trying to make conversation. Nobody knew each other, nobody had anything in common. Conversation would begin, stop, begin again. People would move around trying to find a new chat partner, but the party just wasn't working. Carolyn stood rigidly beside a table of wine bottles and cold cuts. Dr. Price fluttered around filling people's glasses and assuring us that his old girlfriend, a belly dancer, would be here any minute to perform. "A belly dancer?" I thought. "That's ridiculous." Dr. Price seemed very excited about the idea, but nobody else caught his enthusiasm.

One woman on her fourth glass of wine began yelling about Republicans, and several men argued back. Dr. Price put some music on the record player and another lack luster couple began to dance awkwardly. People mumbled at each other, and returned to the cold cuts table stuffing salami and cheese and crackers into their yaps. One woman began to snuffle. And then the belly dancer arrived in all her glory. She wore a coat, which Dr. Price was only too glad to take from her. She was a tired looking, droopy, fifty-year-old with graying hair. She looked edgy and a little nervous as Dr Price took a record album from her and exchanged it for the music already playing. She began to dance slowly and undulate, and all of a sudden, I felt embarrassed for her and for all of us, pretending to be having a good time at this miserable party.

Carolyn was having a conversation, finally, with a pasty faced, fat little man, the belly dancer weaved and bobbed, and a few people sat about watching her and looking glum. The Republicans huddled together, leering at the woman, and the snuffling woman began to give way to downright sobbing while another woman patted her on the back and finally hustled her out of the room. Dr. Price was ignoring me as if I was a stranger. I decided to step outside to have a cigarette and take a breather.

The night air was crisp and the stars were as visible as Christmas tree lights. I wished that I were home in my nightgown and slippers having a sherry before going to bed. But what was I going to do with Carolyn? What if she didn't want to leave, although I couldn't imagine that she was having a good time. But just as I walked back through the door and into the party scene, Carolyn came tromping past me on Dr. Price's arm.

"Oh, Cat," she said, "I have this awful headache, and I couldn't find you, and I asked Dr. Price, if he would mind driving me home."

"You're leaving your own party and driving her home?" I quizzed him.

"Oh, It'll just take a few minutes," he retorted, "besides the belly dancer is going home."

"Pity," I said as the couple scurried away. I downed another small glass of wine and left. I was really annoyed. I was annoyed at Dr. Price for being such a jerk, pretending that I was a piece of the furniture, and I was annoyed at Carolyn for violating the code. Every girl knew by the age of fourteen that you didn't hone in on somebody's else's beau unless you wanted trouble. I mean, he wasn't my beau, in the big sense, but still I felt violated.

"How was the party?" Dorie asked when I came through the door.

"A bust," I said, "about the dullest evening of my life, and wait until I tell you what Carolyn did," but before I could tell her the phone rang. "Who in the hell would be calling at eleven at night?" I asked, taking the receiver off the hook.

Carolyn's whining voice came over the line. "Oh, it's awful, just awful," she began, "Oh what am I going to do?"

"What are you talking about?" I asked, even more annoyed than before.

"Well, it's Dr. Price, I mean he made a pass at me, and I didn't know what to do, and I kissed him back, and now I feel just awful, and I don't know what do."

"Take a hot bath and go to bed," I advised.

"But Cat, I kissed him back."

"Yeah? So?" I said, "Let's talk about this Monday at work," and with that, I hung up. Here was another violation of the code. Not only did you NOT ask someone's beau to take you home from a party, but you didn't lead him on, which I highly suspected she had done, and you never called up your girlfriend and did a mea culpa. It was stupid. Just plain stupid. Dorie and I discussed just how stupid it was for the next hour.

At noon the next day, Dr. Price called acting like nothing had happened. "Did you have a good time last night?" he asked. I should have told him what I thought, but there was that damned code again. You weren't ever to hurt a guy's feelings.

"Oh yes, it was nice," I said. He mealy mouthed around the subject for a few minutes. I knew what he wanted. He wanted to know what I knew about his taking Carolyn home, but passively, I pretended not to get it. When he asked me if I'd like to go to the Pine Cove for a beer later, I told him I was working on report cards and couldn't make it. That little white lie gave me a great deal of satisfaction

The next Monday at school, Carolyn and I were polite but avoided each other. On Wednesday after school, she dragged into my room to tell me that Dr. Price had invited her out to dinner, at the LeFrancois, no less. She had accepted the invitation, but she wanted me to know. There was the code violation again. I told her that she could do what she wanted. I had no claims on the man. The avoidance between

Carolyn and me went of for three weeks, and Dr. Price didn't call. I had just about gotten over my annoyed and hurt feelings when Carolyn called again.

"I could just die," she wailed, "I have to come clean. I slept with Dr. Price!"

"You don't say," I said in a sarcastic voice.

"But I just can't live with myself, and so I called him up and told him that I couldn't see him again, and it wasn't fair to you because you were so in love with him."

"What?" I yelled, "you told him what?"

She began to repeat herself, but I stopped her. "Listen," I began, "you can have him. I don't want him. I am not in love with him. When you came on to him at the party, you left my feelings out. So why are you so concerned about me now anyway?" I demanded.

"Well, I don't know. I'm so confused. I'm going back to my husband. I want to forget all about this," she said, beginning to cry.

"So, I'm some kind of convenient excuse?" I questioned. "I'm your way out?"

"Well, yeah, I guess so," she snuffled. I hung up.

Dorie had come into the room. "You'll never guess what that was all about," I told her.

"Wanna bet?" she said with a disgusted look on her face. "I told you that woman was trouble."

"So, Carolyn's answer to her problems is to make a fool of herself over a man, ruin her relationship with her girlfriend, and go back to the man that beat her. Very onward and upward, isn't it?" I said.

"So what are you going to do about Dr. Price?" Dorie asked.

I thought about it for a moment. "Nothing," I said. "This is none of my business. What Carolyn says is hearsay. I don't want to defend myself or her."

"Good for you," Dorie said. "Let's walk down to the donut shop."

A week later Dr. Price called with his usual invitation to join him for a beer at the Pine Cove. I had nothing better to do. He arrived with a single red rose, which he handed to me saying he had missed me. I just smiled at him and put the rose in water. Neither of us mentioned Carolyn's name in any of our conversation ever again.

The second character in this collection of C's is Claude. I had known him in high school and always had a mad crush on him. He was my boyfriend's best friend and so cute. He had a new Chevy and didn't date much, and was always working on his car. And in those days half of my dates included holding the light over a greasy engine while some guy worked on his car. Oh how I dreamed that he would ask me out, but he never did.

I ran into him in a coffee shop late that fall. He was married, had two children, and had inherited his father's lucrative business. He drove a new Chevy truck. We ordered a second cup of coffee and talked about the old days, and then about my divorce. He said he wasn't that happy with his wife. He said all the things that men say when they are on the make. And some of it I fell for. Why?

Because I wanted to fall for it. All that attention that I never got in high school now was coming my way. It was irresistible.

He began dropping by H Street at odd hours. Dorie didn't like it, and I felt embarrassed. I tried to tell him that coming by at eleven at night and banging on the windows to scare us wasn't cute. But he thought it very funny. He kept showing up, giving us lectures about drinking coffee late at night (which we were), telling us jokes that weren't funny, and then leaving "peeling" out and screeching his tires. Clearly, he never got over high school. He showed off like a sixteen-year-old.

One Sunday afternoon in late October, he stopped by and wanted to know if I wanted to go for a drive down the river road. I had nothing better to do, so I accepted the invitation. He drove for a while, slowing down here and there as if looking for something. He hadn't made a pass, yet I began to get the feeling that he was looking for somewhere to park, and I didn't like it. I tried to talk about the beautiful fall afternoon, and weren't those geese making the "V" high above us wonderful? He muttered and pulled off the road into a secluded orchard. I was about ready to tell him to get back up on the levy road, that I wanted to go home, when I looked from the trees to him. He had his pants unzipped, penis extended, and was jacking off! His eyes were glazed over. It scared the bejasus out of me, and I leaped form the truck and walked back to the main road, not knowing what to do. I felt like I was going to be sick.

Within a few minutes I heard the truck come up behind me, and he pulled over and stopped. I got in and huddled against my door. He said absolutely nothing, and neither did I. We reached H Street and when we stopped for a light two blocks from our duplex, I told him I would get out here.

I walked home, thinking of the crush that I had had on him, thinking how glamorous he seemed in high school and what a jerk he was now ten years later. I got home and told Dorie the story. She wanted to wring his neck, call his wife, put an ad in the newspaper, but what we did instead was put on the coffee pot and talk into the night about the mystery of men.

I was living on H Street with Dorie the night the doorbell rang. Chloe and another girl stood there looking at us. "Just passing through," she told her surprised mother. "This here's Deborah. She's in The Group. We can't travel alone. We have to go in pairs." They came into the living room. Chloe had long dark hair tied up in a bandana. She was wearing a boy's T-shirt, a long skirt and heavy logger-type boots. Deborah was tall and thin with a little rat face half hidden behind thick coke-bottle-lens glasses. She wore a granny dress and rubber thongs. Dorie lit a cigarette, and Deborah sprung into action.

"Put that filthy thing out," she yelled. "It's of the devil."

"This is my house and I'll smoke if I want to," Dorie told her coldly. Deborah left and went to sit on the front steps. Chloe immediately reached for the pack of cigarettes lying on the table and lit up.

They had brought sleeping bags with them, and eventually they bedded down for the night. We didn't know what to expect. The next day we went to work and found them gone when we returned. Gone, too, were some of our things! My favorite record LP was gone, and some of Dorie's clothing was gone as well, as was an especially nice pair of earrings. Grandma was called. No, she didn't know anything about the pair. They had been staying with The Group at the church camp. She hadn't been told that they had left. She went into a howl about the devil having his day, and Dorie hung up.

Several months later, Dorie got a phone call from a remote town in Colorado. Chloe came on the line crying. She and Deborah had made it to this church camp, but she wanted to come home. She was very upset, and Dorie wired her bus fare.

Chloe arrived thin and pale and shaken. When we asked what had happened, she said she didn't want to talk about it. We took her in and fixed her a good meal. Dorie made her a bed on the couch. For the next few days, she appeared paranoid. Every time the phone rang or the mailman put the mail through the slot, she jumped and then cowered into herself. But after a week elapsed, she seemed to be coming out of it. Unfortunately, she made phone calls connecting with her old friends.

It was about that time that Dorie told her that they had to have a talk. What were her plans? Dorie and I had agreed to live as partners for the school year. It wasn't fair to bring someone into the space. We'd all try to make do, but we needed to know what she was thinking. She said she didn't know. Maybe she'd get a job, but another week went by, and we saw no evidence that she was looking for one. And then she began inviting her friends over. We'd come home from work and find the house lousy with those awful teenagers. They'd be playing records so loud that BS and LC called to complain. When we asked them to turn the stereo down, they ignored us. We went to the kitchen to begin fixing dinner and found not a morsel in the house. They had eaten everything or taken it. There wasn't so much as a can of peaches left on the shelf on the service porch. I imagined all my jewelry gone.

Dorie and I went to our bedrooms to survey the scene. Everything seemed in order. In the bathroom, wet towels were piled on the floor, the medicine cabinet had been rifled, the toilet paper was gone, and the soap had disappeared. Someone had taken a mighty shit in the toilet and not flushed. That did it.

"Out!" Dorie commanded from the top of the stairs. "All of you leave immediately and don't come back."

"If my friends go, so do I," Chloe yelled up at her mother.

"Fine," Dorie shrieked as kids began moseying out of the door as if they had all lived through scenes like this before. Chloe was the last to leave, slamming the door behind her. "Oh shit." Dorie said. "I gave her a key."

"Well, we'll just have to change the locks," I said, shaking my head. "You buy the locks down at the hardware store, and I'll start cleaning up their mess." Several hours later, the house was scrubbed and back in order, the records put away in their jackets, and with a big screw driver, we managed to change the door lock. As we put the new keys on our rings, we talked about what on earth to do. We both knew that Chloe would be back. And she was. But Dorie just stood her ground on the front porch and wouldn't let her in. "Not after the last disaster," she told her. "I'll buy you a ticket to Yakima. You figure things out." Chloe had no options, so Dorie drove her to the bus station.

Several weeks later, Dorie got a phone call from her mother saying that Chloe was married; Grandma had arranged it. The boy's name was Tyler, and he came from a church family. The young couple was living with Grandma. She hoped that he'd find a job soon. Grandma hoped that Chloe would get pregnant soon. That would settle her down. Dorie was devastated by the news. That playful, lovely child had gone through the family metamorphosis, and she'd be as trapped as the rest of them had been.

Grandma sent a snapshot taken on Chloe's wedding day. There she stood wearing a shapeless, short white dress looking miserable. Beside her was a long haired boy grinning.

Counselors and
Carousel Sex

Dorie and I both made friends with counselors, wise, father like men that we trusted. Dorie met her counselor at American River College, and I met mine at Sacramento State University. It was amazing how much our experiences were alike. First there was the student-counselor relationship, then a friendship developed, and then there was seduction. These professional men turned our friendship into an opportunity for seduction. And when all was said and done, we felt violated and incredibly stupid.

I think their attention was such a turn-on because we both had very distant fathers. We longed for our father's attention and approval, but our mothers saw to it that we didn't get it. Little girls were to keep to themselves and their female relations and leave boys and their fathers alone. That was a strict code of behavior in our rural backgrounds. When husbands finally came our way, we had been told by them, "No other man would ever want us. We were lucky that they had married us." And at some level, we believed them. What a turn-on, then, when these older, professional men found us desirable.

Our trysts with these men had happened before we lived together on H Street. We never told anyone about them, but on H Street, everything about our past came out. We trusted each other. We could tell each other our secrets. We could analyze what had happened. We could try to figure it out together. There was no shame or blame attached to our stories. We wanted to understand; that was all.

In some regards our stories were funny. After trying to seduce the very confused Dorie for some weeks, all the counselor could do was exhibit his limp organ and thump at it with his fingers. Dorie lay undressed on his couch looking on at the thing, horrified. And then said counselor got down on his knees and began doing push-ups, huffing and puffing away. Dorie got dressed and left. She had talked to this man several times a week for a year. She had told him everything about her ex-husband and Chloe, her relationship with her mother, savior and ogre, she had described her dreams, and she had warmed to his advances. And now this embarrassing display! It was appalling. She never spoke to him again. She felt naïve and very, very ashamed.

When I heard her story, I commiserated. My counselor experience had been almost exactly the same. The counseling, the friendship, and the seduction, which just didn't work out. When I finally succumbed to my counselor in the front seat of his van, he couldn't get it up either. I, too, had felt horrified at his behavior and at mine I didn't see him again either, but he continued to make obscene phone calls to me for months. Then something more than sordid stories began to emerge from our conversations. And that is what we eventually called Carousel Sex.

We had been raised with a strict sexual code of behavior. Nobody explained anything about our bodies or sex to us. But the code said sex could only happen between married people. To let a boy put his hands on you previous to marriage was a dirty thing. It made you a slut and no respectable boy would ever propose. Nobody explained just deep, overwhelming sexual feelings. You weren't supposed to have those feelings before marriage evidently. But, of course, we did.

So, every time you had a crush on a boy, you imagined marriage. Any kissing or petting session, which was promoted by those boys, had to be compartmentalized into a pre-wedding experiment. Otherwise, we couldn't live with our guilt. And so we married early and were very respectable, but miserable and unhappy. We had married unwisely. And all the respectability in the world couldn't make up for it. There had to be more than the married life we experienced. We saw other women going out into the world doing things that we wished we could do, like going to college, for instance. Why couldn't we go? It was almost free, and entrance tests said we were bright enough. But our husbands disagreed. We were supposed to stay home and fix their dinners, wash their clothes, and be ready at their beck and call to do our married duty with them even if by now, it was mechanical and boring and they didn't seem to understand that our souls needed romance and genuine caring. Dorie's husband was a philanderer and mine was a workaholic. We didn't count for much.

But as newly single women, we began to experience a whole new world, one alive with the possibilities of love affairs. We still had to imagine marriage as a final result, but that view was becoming more and more anemic. Men and love affairs came and went. Shameful experiences that made us nauseous came and went, such as mine with Claude, or ours with those counselors. We began to make jokes about men and their sexuality. We began to doubt their power after all. And we began to talk about carousel sex.

It came about one afternoon when we talked about the counselors again. "I think," Dorie said, "that my sexual feelings are just like riding on a carousel. Remember what it was like? You climbed onto the wooden horse, and the whole thing began going around and around and the horse went up and down, and you just were spinning in so many different directions, up and down, around and around. Your psyche just moved into a magical place of movement, of time and space. And when the ride stopped, it was hard to climb down from the horse and return to the solid ground. Remember the colors of the carousel, the music, the movement of pure joy? Well, that's what unencumbered, letting go, joyful sex is like. Why does it have to be slam/bam, its over, or attached to some expectation of engagement or marriage? Why can't a woman just have a totally joyful experience and move on. Hell, perhaps you don't even know the guy's name. Who cares? And when it happens, we're not sluts. We're not dirty. We're not going to hell or any of the other things the preachers and our mothers told us. Why shouldn't we be liberated from the constraints of the past, the lies our society tried to cram down our throats? Why can't we be sexual beings that just love life, and romping about in bed is part of the glory of being alive?"

I listened, stunned, enchanted. She was right. Why couldn't we live our lives that way? Why couldn't we be as free as men to glory in sex if we wanted to, providing no one got hurt, no one misunderstood, and no married men ever again! No more. We would scrutinize men more carefully from now on for their obvious lies about their marital status. We would talk more and more about developing a personal ethic where our sexuality was concerned. No more little girls hammered by our mother's rules. All those rigid rules of the past were going in the garbage can. We would replace them with new ones that fit this new age. We would triumph!

But damn, for all our fine talk, we had no idea how hard it was going to be!

$\mathcal{D}$

DIETS

Give us this day our daily bread

But help us from gobbling so much!

To diet or not to diet: that was the question. To gorge on cole slaw and French fries or to sip white wine and eat a green salad sans dressing. To begin the day at Sambo's and a stack of pancakes, or to face the day with a soft boiled egg and black coffee. That was the decision that had to be made. It was an arduous decision. It took strength of character and an iron will. We wanted to be svelte and glamorous as the media told us we should be. If you were thin, it seemed, all of your problems went away. Men followed you home from bus stops and asked you to fly to Monte Carlo with them, the president of the college asked you to be his chief aide, and Harpers Bazaar called upon you to model the latest fashions.

But in our minds, we weren't thin, or thin enough. Dorie probably weighed 130 lbs. and I weighed 120. Anybody listening to our talk of diets would have thought us nuts. But media had convinced us that we were too fat. We decided to begin our latest diet with a fast. A three day fast to get us off to a good start.

The first day, we lay about the house moaning, too weak to so much as lift a book or dust mop. By the second day, we began to perk up, feel the exhilaration of the challenge as our bodies began to pull carbohydrates out of our pudgy little cells. We discussed the philosophy of fasting, of John the Baptist eating only locust and honey in the wilderness. This fasting must be good for the soul, for how could a soul develop if it was weighted down with cheeseburgers and banana cream pie?

On the third day, we allowed ourselves a simple glass of grapefruit juice. How our taste buds responded! It was glorious. Later on, we allowed ourselves a hard-boiled egg and three glasses of water. We asked each other if we should use salt on our egg, and then we decided against it. Salt made you retain water and that made you look fat.

On the fourth day, we allowed ourselves a green salad with no dressing and a broiled hamburger patty. The scales actually plunged downward by a pound or two. We were triumphant. And so we decided to celebrate. We had earned it. We would go to Capitol Tamale, one of our favorite restaurants, and order a steak and salad. Well, perhaps one piece of their garlic bread. It was their specialty. Perhaps just one small piece.

On the fifth day toward sundown, we took the no. 25 bus downtown and got off at 10th and L. We walked a half a block to the restaurant. We entered, waited to be seated, and gave each other a superior smile when we were asked if we'd like a drink from the bar while we waited. Oh no, they couldn't catch us up with that little ploy. Our game plan included one glass of wine – not drinks from the bar. Finally, we were seated.

Then the wonderful smells began coming from the kitchen. We noted the sumptuous dishes other people around us were enjoying. One thing led to another, and before you knew it, we had consumed two margaritas and two champagne cocktails with strawberries. We devoured a whole basket of hot, buttery garlic bread. I had a bowl of beef broth, a green salad with blue cheese dressing, and a mound of raviolis. Dorie had a beef broth, a salad with oil and vinegar, a fillet of sole, and a big lump of mashed potatoes. We both had a chocolate éclair for dessert.

We left the place gluttonous wrecks, ruined, ashamed, and considered ourselves unredeemable.

The next morning, we could hardly face each other. We avoided contact. I stayed in the shower an hour and a half. But eventually, we both arrived at the work table in the dining room and decided that we had to talk. "We had been really, really hungry," we told each other. After an hour of discussion and mutual confessions, we decided that new tactics were in order.

Exercise! Now that was the thing that had been lacking from our first plan. If only we would exercise, everything would regain balance. So, we planned to continue with grapefruit, eggs, green salads and hamburger patties, but each night we would take a long walk. That very night we started off a brisk clip and ended up at the all night donut shop where we downed a jelly donut.

Well, obviously we had walked in the wrong direction. The next night we walked the other way, but found ourselves in front of the ice cream parlor. I had a lemon custard cone and Dorie chocolate.

It was clear that we were failures at the diet game. To truly diet, you had to cancel those little Friday suppers out, those Sunday morning waffles, the ice cream cone at the end of a walk. In short, you had to stop eating everything that gave you pleasure, live with the pain of starvation, and stay cooped up like a hermit. A social life meant eating and drinking. How did those top models do it? They did it, we learned, by taking diet pills on a regular basis, which killed a goodly number of them off. Dexatrim, which was advertised in all the magazines and on TV was addictive, ruined your teeth and could stop your heart. We were smart enough to decide to avoid it and all the over the counter pills just like it. We would just have to live with the idea that we were a size six and eight.

"Look at BS," I told Dorie one day. "She seems to accept her size completely. I never hear of her going on a diet. She's so secure about herself. Let's ask her how that happened."

"How you gonna do that," Dorie quipped. "How you gonna say, 'Gee, Kate, you're a big girl yet you don't seem to care.' Won't that be insulting?"

"Yeah, not very sensitive," I answered. "You're right." But several days later, we got our answer. BS and LC were over for fruit pudding and coffee one evening when we got on the subject of diets. BS just sat there listening and smiling at our stories. Then she said the most amazing thing.

"Chocolate cake," she began, "you know every Saturday of my life that I can remember, I made my Dad a chocolate layer cake with frosting. That was his favorite. He'd come in from doing the usual Saturday yard work, shower, and Mom would fix dinner. And then, I'd bring that cake out of the pantry, and set it in the middle of the table. Dad always went on and on about how wonderful it looked, and at how skilled I was at baking. Then he'd pour coffee and I'd cut the cake, and we'd all ooh and ahh over it. Mom and I never thought about our waist lines. All that mattered was how much Dad appreciated that cake. He said that I'd make some man very happy some day with my ability to bake a cake like that. I know that I'm taller and wider than lots of girls… well, look at June here, but I'm athletic and solid and big boned, an Amazon Dad used to call me. That was meant as special praise. So, I'm never going to worry about my weight."

We all nodded and smiled at her story. LC shrugged and said nobody in her family was fat even though they were raised on pasta and sour dough sandwiches. She thought she had good genes. They both laughed at our belief that we were too fat. After they left, we sat down to talk about the obvious. "So, I think that if your Dad thought you were the center of the universe, his little princess, your body image is probably realistic and balanced. And if you didn't have that kind of relationship with your Dad, or a stand in of any type, you may have a distorted image. Right?"

"Psychology 1A," Dorie said sipping her coffee. "So my question is, if you didn't have a 'present' father figure, and you do have a distorted image egged on by TV and magazines, how do you get over it? Counseling?" and with that we both laughed.

"Maybe with a woman counselor," I said.

"Or maybe if you have any insight about yourself, you just work on it inside your own head or talk with a girlfriend," Dorie said.

"Or write about it in your journal," I said. And then we explored things we could do to change our mirror image for the next two hours.

ℰ

EWELL

Ewell was one of those good black men, good because he was somebody, and good because he kept reminding everyone that he was somebody. Like Sidney Poitier, he was the kind of black man that you invited home to dinner, and so we did.

Ewell was a poet in residence at the college, and Dorie had had the opportunity to have coffee with him and discuss the state of modern poetry. Dorie was enchanted with his views. So we carefully planned a little dinner party inviting about ten people from the English department that might enjoy an evening with the poet. Ewell arrived promptly. He was a handsome man, dressed very carefully for the occasion. He sat in the rocking chair in our living room, looking quite magnificent. Dorie poured him a glass of wine, and the other guests began to arrive.

We served a buffet supper of broiled herb chicken, rice pilaf, and steamed asparagus. Everyone was congenial. Ewell began telling stories about his early life in Chicago, and everyone laughed at appropriate moments. Then Professor Fred began telling stories about his graduate school days that I'd heard a dozen times, and his wife added stories about their three children, and how they were coping with raising the little rascals. Old Alice Summering told us she had just found a book of poetry from an obscure sixteenth century Dutch poet. Herman Schmidt wrung his hands and complained of the quality of student essays these days. Dave Norton made quips in Spanish, his specialty, and Arthur Landers griped about the amount of committee work you were expected to do these days. How on earth could you write a novel, he wondered when you had to teach three classes and serve on all those committees? Everybody nodded and clucked. Ewell said that grading student papers was getting in his way of writing poetry. All those guest appearances and work shops in modern poetry were slowing him down, and everyone commiserated.

And then just as Dorie was serving the coffee and I was dishing out the fruit pudding, that awful Ruby Hanson interrupted and said she'd brought along a record album special for the occasion. She whipped the vinyl disc out of its sleeve and put it on our stereo. It was some kind of interview of some black activist who in ghetto slang kept saying how much he hated whitey, and how the time had come to "get him." Ewell went rigid as did everyone else. Ruby was enjoying the scene immensely.

We should have leaped up, taken the damn thing off the stereo and apologized for Ruby's choice of entertainment. But nobody knew what to do, so we all just sat there feeling embarrassed and looking at our laps. Finally, the awful thing was over, and I turned off the stereo and tried to say something intelligent. But nothing much came forth. "What do you think, Ewell," Ruby said, leaning toward him, "about the message this young man is sending out?"

"Well, I don't know," he stuttered. "I mean there are some in the black community that unfortunately feel that way, but the majority of us..." and he trailed off. People began standing up, grabbing at their coats and handbags, making leaving noises. Here we had all been so modern having a pleasant evening with a black man in our midst, thinking how much we were alike, congratulating ourselves on our progressive attitudes, and then Ruby had brought that awful record into our midst reminding us all that we were different, that there was still terrible trouble in our world between white and black people. Everyone left with troubled faces.

Dorie wanted to kill Ruby Hanson, and I didn't blame her. She plotted how to destroy her for the next few days. She said she'd never invite her to another party as long as she lived. And then Dorie went to see Ewell to apologize. He was gracious and kind and said not to worry about it. Actually, he'd been working on a poem with Dorie in mind, and he whipped out a piece of paper and began to recite. It was a beautiful poem about a black goddess deep in a jungle in Africa, filled with symbolic meaning and little riffs of enthusiasm. Dorie couldn't figure out what it had to do with her, but she stayed in his office talking for an hour, and then he invited her to come over to his apartment for drinks, and he held her hand on the way to his complex, and after three vodkas and limes, he said that sharing poetry with her was so meaningful to him and then one thing led to another, and he began sharing with her all right! Dorie was flat on her back and Ewell was flailing away on top.

Well, she came home late that night, and I could tell by the way she looked, that she'd experienced some great romantic interlude. "Oh, this man was wonderful," she said. "Oh the soul of a poet, the ancient beauty of his voice, the language that came out of his consciousness. Oh my!"

"Umha," I thought.

Well, a week went by and then two weeks, and she neither saw him on campus nor did he call. Well, you couldn't expect a poet to be socially or romantically conscious like a train conductor. He was obviously engrossed in great metaphors and silvery similes. He probably was busy with production schedules for his next book or poetry reading in the community. Yes, he must be quite busy.

By the third week, Dorie was angry. Was he just another rogue who sweet-talked you into bed and then forgot all about you? How dare he do her this way. Carousel sex was forgotten. He had said she really mattered to him. She would track him down, and so she found him one late afternoon sitting behind his desk in his office. She walked through the door and stood in front of it. He couldn't escape. He nervously fingered several wooden pencils, his eyes flitted here and there, sweat began to run down into his collar.

"I just wanted to tell you that I don't enjoy being used," she began. "I thought we had a great deal in common. I loved our talks about poetry and, well, everything, and then that night at your apartment, well, I thought…"

"Oh, that!" he squeaked in a high inauthentic voice. He was saved by a phone call. "Yes? Oh yes, I'll be right there," he gushed. He stood up and said he'd forgotten an appointment and had to go immediately. He rushed out of the door leaving a trail of broken pencils behind him.

Dorie sat down in the chair across from his desk. Here it was again. The great black poet in residence, with all his publications and honors and prestige. And her, little Dorie McKenzie from Yakima, WA, who had no notoriety in her life, had scared the bejasus out of him.

Was it the same old theme we talked about where men felt threatened by passionate women, afraid their very juices might be sucked out of them and they'd die? Or did he, just like the many white men we'd met, love the seduction for what it was, love the literal sex, and had no more use for a woman after the act was completed? Had he revealed too much of himself with her and didn't want to be reminded of it? If we believed in carousel sex, why were her feelings so hurt? Dorie saw a piece of paper on top of a pile of his things on his desk. One line was written. It seemed like the beginning of a new poem. It read: "I am a black missionary in this land of sterile white."

"Oh no, you're not," she thought. You're just another lowdown, shagging shit head!" And she left his office to come home and tell me all about it.

$\mathcal{F}$

FIRE AND FROGS

There she stood in her front yard with her purse and Bible under her arm, and two pair of clean underpants in her hands, watching her house burn to the ground. Hot, shooting flames of fire shot toward the sky, and that heat paralleled her own coldness. In this tale of H Street, F surely stands for fire.

It had all started the night before when we had come home from eating out, and I had been quite nervous. I paced the floor and smoked one cigarette after another, and couldn't calm down. I felt extremely distraught. I didn't know where this was coming from, but I felt as if something terrible was about to happen.

"Is it Joe?" Dorie asked.

"No, it's someone close to home," I said with a frown.

We decided to write down the time of my prophecy. It was eleven twenty P.M. We went to bed, but I didn't get to sleep until three a.m..

We got up at seven as usual when the phone rang. We looked at each other. There was no good news coming from an early morning call. I picked up the receiver.

"Cat!" my friend Diana cried into the phone. "My house burned down last night. Nothing left. Everything gone!"

"What?" I shrieked.

66

"God, don't yell so early in the morning," Dorie barked. It was the first time that Dorie had yelled at me, and I felt as if she had slapped me across the face. I felt humiliated by her disapproval. It almost was more important than the news of Diana's burning house. Abruptly, I turned toward the phone so that Dorie wouldn't see the tears forming in my eyes. I listened as Diana told her story.

Dorie hovered near wondering what the phone call was about and feeling guilty for lashing out. "Diana's house burned down," I mouthed toward her.

"Oh my god," she mouthed back, going into the kitchen to fix scrambled eggs and cinnamon orange slices just the way I loved them.

I called my school and ordered a substitute and drove out to what had been my friend's house. Her brother, Steve, the crazy one who had showed up when Joe and I had landed in Sacramento, had set the house on fire. He had crawled up on the roof, probably higher than a kite, doused the wooden shingles with gasoline, and lit a match. Poof! It was a good fire. He had scrambled down off the roof, then thought better of what he had done and gotten out the garden hose and tried to spray water on the fire, but it was too hot, going too strong, for the squirt from a mere garden hose to stop it.

Diana, her two children, and her mother lived together in the house. She had heard a scratching sound seemingly coming from the wall right before she went to bed. She couldn't sleep because of the noise, and for some reason went to investigate the closet where it seemed to be coming from. When she opened the closet door, flames flashed out. She grabbed and ran, screaming at her mother and children to get outside while she called the fire department.

The fire engines arrived and the crewmen began their work, but the fire was a fast one, and most of the house was ruined before they got the fire out. At this point, Steve emerged from the back yard where he had watched the spectacle asking the fire crew if anyone had a cigarette. A short conversation with the "weirdo" made the firemen suspicious and the police were called. The last Diana saw of her brother, he was handcuffed and placed in the back seat of the police car. The two women and children just stood there stunned, until a friendly neighbor asked if there was anyone that they wanted to call. Diana called me.

Now, I stood with my friends looking at the ruin and wondering what to do. Diana's mother had called her insurance agent, and the Red Cross had already assigned the family a motel room not far away. The fire people suggested that they go to the motel for the rest of the day. Meet their agent there. Order some sandwiches in. "Have a few cold ones," the fire chief said.

Diana and the chief looked at each other. She smiled, he flirted, he handed her his card. Right then and there, another romance was born which was to last off and on for two years.

"Who finds romance at the end of a fireman's hose?" Dorie asked when hearing the story.

"Only my friend, Diana," I said, "and you want to rethink that last line?" We collapsed into laughter.

Well, it was some months later, when the construction crew was rebuilding the house, and Diana's love affair with the fire chief was hot and heavy, that she saw the tiny green frog in the lumber pile in the back yard of the property. She decided that the frog must mean good luck, and she told me all about it.

And I told Dorie.

"You ever make a bean bag frog?" she asked.

"Never," I said.

"They're kinda fun, used to make them for Chloe when she was little. I still got the pattern around here somewhere."

Dorie found the pattern. "It's simple," she said. " It's just the body of a frog shaped thing, with four splayed legs, and a big head." We cut the crathur out of velvet scraps, stitched it up leaving a spoon sized opening between its back legs and the filled it with small white dried beans. We did the final stitch, and then sewed on buttons for eyes, and tied a ribbon around its neck. It was cute as could be. I gave one to Diana, to her mom, and to her kids.

And then we really got into it, making frogs. We discussed who was frog worthy and who wasn't. It wasn't just anybody that should have a frog. I made one for my friend Charlotte, a really eccentric sharp woman who had been my boss when I worked for the California Resources library while going to school. I even added small pearl "balls" between the hind legs, saying in the card that accompanied it, "to a woman who has more balls than anyone I know." She was delighted.

I made a red velvet frog for Evor Price, who acted like nobody had ever given him anything before.

"Well," he said, plopping the thing from one hand to another. "Well, well, well."

I finally took it away from him and laid it on his coffee table before he plopped the thing silly, broke it open, and spilled beans all over the floor.

One night about midnight, I awakened to the call of my name. Dorie stood in the bedroom doorway with a flash light shining into the darkness of the room.

"What is it," I asked sleepily

"I've been thinking," she said, "Simon shall have no frog!" And with that she went back to her room.

Simon? No frog?

"Well, I swan," I thought, as we used to say in Humboldt, Iowa.

The next morning over coffee, Dorie explained. Simon North, Dr. Simon North, was our mentor and friend. He had taken Dorie under his wing, gotten her a T.A. job teaching English 1A, and approved her master's thesis. He was beautiful, elegant, old world, brilliant, charming, and genuinely interested in our welfare. But early on, romance between Simon and Dorie had blossomed. Or it hadn't blossomed. We could never figure out which. He acted as if he was her mentor. Then he acted as if he was courting her. And the he feigned disinterest. It was a roller coaster ride. And he was married.

It was the strangest marriage. Neither of us had ever heard of such a thing. Two people are married for over twenty years. They share a lovely home. He teaches at the university, and she runs a public relations company in a city four hundred miles away. She spends about half of the year in the other city. They are absolutely committed to each other; they both have affairs on the side. Never heard of such a thing!

Once again, Simon had totally confused Dorie by his actions and confidential talk of his wife. Therefore, she'd had enough, and Simon would have no frog. It was very fitting, I agreed.

And so during a short period of time, Diana's house burned down, Steve went to jail, Diana began an affair with a married fire captain, and we began the business of frog making. Secretly, I knew that Dorie made Simon a blue satin frog with crystal eyes, but it remained in her room on her dresser. Simon never got his frog.

$\mathcal{G}$

GARAGE SALE

They came leaping over the boxes, they came leaping over the racks, they came leaping through the open doors, they came leaping through the cracks! They were everywhere, mauling, bickering and rummaging for goods. We had decided to have a garage sale. Little did we know what we were in for.

One day Dorie and I decided to sort though all our junk, all that stuff that accumulated, all that stuff packed in boxes in closets that we'd been carting around with us for years. We wanted to be rid of all of it. BS and LC agreed to add their stuff and help. So, we put an ad in the paper for a garage sale on a Saturday morning and began to sort through all those boxes, sacks, and piles of stuff. We got up extra early and were just beginning to arrange things on the front porch and lawn, when people began arriving. It was six thirty a.m. BS and LC were still in bed.

"Our sale doesn't begin until eight," we said. Nobody paid any attention. They began pawing through what we had set out. Folks began pouring in to plunder, debate, and buy. An elderly woman insisted on buying the box on the front porch for two dollars. Actually, it was a box into which we had sorted things that were too trivial to sell, a real junk box that would go into the garbage. But the old one glommed onto it. What did she want with a few odd buttons, broken zippers, ruined Christmas tree ornaments, and the extra slats to a bed, long ago hauled to the dump? She slapped two dollars into my hand, and made off with the treasure.

A fat woman bought an old skillet for fifty cents, and then crammed her bulk through our front door to begin rummaging around in our kitchen cabinets. Dorie caught her at it, and shoved her back outside, where she cackled, went to her car, and waved one of our good kitchen knives at us as she drove away.

It was an odd observation, but everyone looked as if they were wearing crappy clothes that they'd bought at a previous garage sale. Women with dry, flat hair pulled back into pony tails with rubber bands climbed out of Okie cars. Men with furtive eyes asked if we had any tools. Pale, pinched-faced children scattered about looking for toys. They were professional garage sale people, we were told by one observer, people that made most of their living by buying our stuff and then selling it at their homes hoping to make a profit. We actually caught one guy who had bought a box of old clay pots, half of them nicked or broken down one side, selling the same box to a newcomer who had just pulled up.

And everyone haggled. One man picked up a pair of rabbit ears.

"Whadaya wan for this," he whined.

"One dollar," Dorie said.

"Oh no you don't, your'en not gonna gyp me that way," he said, "I'll give ya thirty-five cents."

Dorie grabbed back the rabbit ears and threw them onto a table, glaring at the man. It was only nine thirty, but already we both had about had it.

Old ladies, especially, wanted baby clothes. What were they going to do with them? Did they have a raggedy pack of grandchildren somewhere?

"Have any baby clothes?," one woman asked.

"No, no baby clothes," I answered.

"Well, why not, a young woman like you and all," she said, insulting my maternal history.

If we didn't have what they wanted, they seemed disgusted, angry, as if we had tricked them into coming.

"Steak knives""

"No, no steak knives."

"Wall, I niver hear'd of a garage sale that don't have no steak knives," I was told.

I noticed a little, bald man lurking around. He had small childlike hands as he pawed through a few things, but he kept looking around in a funny way. Later, I found him in the basement where we had furniture and a few boxes stored that we did not want to get rid of.

"What are you doing down here," I demanded.

"Best stuff is in the basement," he smiled with a reptile presence.

"Well, anything in the basement is off-limits," I said. "Now please leave." He shambled up the steps and disappeared into the crowd.

"Where have all these people come from?" BS and LC asked, while trying to keep a close watch on the cupcake pan into which they sorted coins. Paper money was put in an envelope underneath the pan. And people just kept coming.

There was the woman who bought a broken bicycle seat. There was the Chinese man who haggled over an electric drill set. Dorie wanted five dollars for it, and he was determined to pay three fifty.

"But I can buy sets like these at the Good Will for three fifty any day of the week," he reasoned.

"Good. Go to the Good Will," she yelled at him.

"Can't because they are all out," he yelled back. " I want this drill set for three fifty!"

We saved mayonnaise jars, pickle jars, jam jars. It was a throwback to the days our depression-raised mothers came from families that threw nothing away. We had about fifty jars sitting on the porch steps. Al of a sudden, I heard a crash. A teenager, a wan girl with dead eyes, had been making pyramids of them, and half of them had come crashing down.

"Whoops," she said, walking away.

I got the broom and began sweeping up broken glass. Next, I watched her thump a small jar of beads left over from some craft project as she walked by. Tiny beads went flying out over the lawn never to be found again. I glared at her back as she sauntered down the street. BS and LC continued to take money, separating all four accounts so we'd each get exact money for our stuff.

The final awful incident happened about two twenty in the afternoon. A small, ancient woman we called Grandma Spider declared that she would buy the pair of rollaway beds for fifteen dollars. She only lived a few blocks away. How would an old woman like herself get those two beds home? She looked to us for an answer, but we hadn't any. Next, she said that if we would sell her the beds for thirteen dollars then she'd have two dollars to give to some guy with a pickup truck to deliver them to her home. She wrung her hand and muttered about company coming and you couldn't expect people to sleep on the floor. She really needed those beds. She paced around, but about every five minutes she'd ask one of us if thirteen dollars would be acceptable for those beds. We were holding strong for fifteen dollars.

About a half hour later, two muscular young men parked at the curb.

"Got any tools?" one of them asked.

We shook our heads, just as Grandma Spider rushed to their truck waving her hands in delight. She kept turning and pointing toward the beds. Dorie took the money into the house for safekeeping, and I began to consolidate the few leftovers on various card tables.

"Well," Grandma Spider said to me, "those boys are going to load up those beds. For fifteen dollars. O.K. boys." The two young men loaded the beds up on their truck, and pulled away with the treasure.

"Oh my, I'd better hurry along," Grandma Spider said. "They'll be waiting for me. Here, dear, here's the money… Oh my, oh my! I gave those boys two dollars and I guess all I have left is thirteen dollars after all. Beds are gone now. Guess you'll have to take my thirteen dollars." She laid the money on a card table and quickly skipped away.

"That miserable old crook," I thought.

We took in the card tables, leaving what hadn't sold out on the lawn, hoping that thieves would take it away during the night. We were right, by the next morning almost everything was gone. The four of us counted our loot. Altogether we'd made over $300. Not bad, we reckoned, but we agreed that having a garage sale was a gruesome task, and whenever something halfway broke or began to look shabby, I would say, "Save it for the next garage sale," and then we'd all laugh, roll our eyes, and throw it directly into the garbage. None of us had the heart to ever have a garage sale again.

$\mathcal{H}$
HOUSEWORK

We were such tidy souls. Neither of us could stand a dirty house, but cleaning took up so much good reading time! We decided that cleaning would take less time if we got organized. I would clean the bathroom and vacuum. Dorie would clean the kitchen and scrub the floor. We would clean every Saturday morning. We would pick up every evening before we went to bed. And of course, neither of us would think of leaving dirty dishes in the sink.

One Saturday morning as I was scouring away at the bathroom, I realized that it needed a good renovation. The floor was the old-fashioned nickel-sized hexagon shaped white tile. The walls were painted except with steam from the shower, about half of the paint looked bubbled and cracked or was literally peeling off. The tiles around the tub were in decent shape although they were hard to keep clean, their glaze having worn off ages ago. The tub's bottom had much of the porcelain worn away and there were rust spots in places. Even though I used gallons of bleach in the tub, it never looked really clean. The sink and stool were newer additions to the bathroom and in pretty good shape.

So we bought a nice blue rug and shower curtain, hung an abstract painting of a balloon seller on the wall above the toilet, and with good towels and a few ivy plants on the window ledge, the bathroom looked decent enough. There wasn't much we could do about the crumbling paint.

The bath had one good-sized glazed window with a brass handle which when turned cranked the window open. The view was the neighbor's back yard, a real secret garden. It appeared oval in shape with a lovely thick carpet of green grass, myriad bushes and shrubs all pruned to perfection and a twelve inch border of pink flowers adjacent to the fences. An old, full pine tree stood to one side of the yard. It was just beautiful, a park. But the funny thing was that I never saw anyone working in it, watering, planting, pruning. It was as if the faeries attended it during the night.

Down in the kitchen, the ceiling was cracked and beginning to bulge downward. The bathroom was directly over it. Dorie could just see entertaining her best beau at the dinner table a few feet away from the kitchen, when the tub with me ensconced would come crashing through the ceiling. I could just see myself stark naked with shower cap on my head picking myself up from the wreckage of the plaster, splintered wood, and broken porcelain.

"Oh yes, Sidney," she'd say, "have you met my roommate, Cat?"

As I cleaned the bathroom, I would hear Dorie singing to herself as she scrubbed the kitchen floor. The house would smell of soap and lemon-scented furniture polish. Within an hour, everything would be sparkling.

"Got any apple turnovers?" I'd ask, knowing that we always kept some in the freezer. We'd bake the turnovers, put the coffee pot on, and put away our cleaning supplies. We would begin one of our endless conversations about men, and then Dorie would usually suggest that we get out of the house for awhile. We'd walk to the park, or take the A bus downtown to the movies, carefully locking up that warm, sweet nest behind us.

I

ITALIAN STEVE AND
ISIAH COOPER

Italian Steve was wild and fiery and quite a shit. Just the type for Dorie to fall in love with. The story of Italian Steve has a beginning, a middle, and a very wicked end.

The beginning of the story takes place at the college where she met him in a graduate class. Before long, they were having coffee dates. Then coffee stretched into long lunches and dates for quiet dinners at out of the way restaurants. Steve always paid. He taught Spanish at some high school while he worked on his degree. He spoke Italian Spanish, and French, besides English. He was very European in outlook and manners. I remember having a conversation about "not scaring this guy off by going to bed with him." No more wild plungings. No more romantic visions. No casual sex.

But a few days after having this conversation, Dorie came home from a picnic at the lake with that certain disheveled look that could only mean one thing.

Well, I was having my own problems with Evor Price, again. I wasn't about to give Dorie any advice or remind her of her commitment to sensible actions.

Two days after the picnic episode, he stood Dorie up for a date. He had planned a movie date. He would pick her up at seven. She waited until eight to call his apartment, but no one answered the phone. There was nothing to do but go to bed early and wonder what had happened.

The next day, Dorie was frustrated beyond words. What had happened to the date? Why no phone call? She had conversation after conversation with him about trust issues They had been in agreement about those issues. She had bought a new dress. And now this had happened. Damn! We agreed that for all this big talk, he must be just another scared rabbit. We had just seen <u>Anne of A Thousand Days</u>. There it was, Anne fending off Henry VIII and keeping his attention and ardor. Once she gave in to him, he lost interest. It was the beginning of her grisly end. We commiserated with her character. There it was. The caution that our mother's had given us. We didn't want to admit that they were right, but here was the evidence, once again.

Evor Price took me out for a beer a few evenings later, and when we arrived back on H Street, I recognized Steve's car out in front. I told Price good night, and made a lot of noise coming through the front door. I didn't want to come upon a "scene." But the only scene in evidence was Steve and Dorie sipping coffee at the dining room table. I excused myself and went up to my room.

The next day I got the story. It seemed that Steve's old girl friend, Beth, had showed up in his life on the very night that he was supposed to take Dorie to the movies. She was down on her luck, broke, and had nowhere to go. Even though they'd been broken up for a year, he had taken her back in "just until she could get on her feet."

"I mean, we're not sleeping together or anything," he assured Dorie.

He made another date for the next night. Seven. Movie. Right. But again, he never showed or called. Now, we both were furious.

"I'm going over to his apartment and tell the asshole off once and for all," Dorie raged.

"You're what?" I asked.

"I'm telling him off! All this mealy-mouthed story about some ex-girlfriend! I deserve a phone call if he can't make a date. A god damned phone call. You coming with me?" she asked.

"Wouldn't miss this for the world," I said.

We drove to Steve's apartment complex. His car was in his parking space, and lights were on in his apartment. I stood at the bottom of the stairs while Dorie marched to the top and began pounding on the door. Nothing. She pounded some more.

"Come out of there, you son of a bitch," she yelled. "I know you're home."

The door parted just a inch or two.

"You can't come in," Steve said, holding a towel around his ass.

"Oh yes I can," Dorie growled, pushing the door and Steve out of the way. The bedroom door was open, and Dorie marched through it, only to find the lovely Beth (we presumed) sitting up in bed, looking back at her wide-eyed. Steve slunk back to the bed, crawled in beside Beth and covered himself head and all with the quilt.

"What's your business, lady," Beth squeaked out.

"What's yours?" Dorie shot back. "All I want from him is a decent phone call when he can't make a date he's set with me. That's all. Just a fucking phone call. I don't deserve to be stood up, not by him or anyone else."

"Oh…could I make you a cup of tea or something?" Beth asked.

"No, I don't want a cup of fucking tea," Dorie stormed. "I just want to tell him that he is a son of a bitch." And with that, she turned and left the apartment.

"Wow," I said in wonder on the way home. "You sure told him off! I'm proud of you."

"No more slinking around, waiting for the phone to ring," she said. "I'm through with all of this crap!"

Of course, Italian Steve never called on Dorie again. And I don't think Dorie grieved for him for one minute. Her self-respect and anger had saved her for one of the first times in her life, and it felt powerful and good. Some months later, she saw Italian Steve sitting in the faculty dining room, holding hands with some wide-eyed co-ed, definitely not Beth, who was looking into his eyes and cooing.

"Oh, brother!" Dorie said, telling me the story. "Does that girl have a rude awakening ahead of her…the son of a bitch. Couldn't even give me a decent phone call."

It was about this time that BS began dating a man named Isiah Cooper. He was a park ranger and wore a uniform much like hers. They'd met at a department meeting where she'd given a report on some kind of bug currently invading the forests, and they'd had a beer that evening to continue talking about it. Isiah was a big man, tall and strong and plain. There was nothing flashy or fiery about him. His voice was clear and direct, but he never told preposterous stories or whined about his job. His family lived in Marysville where he'd been raised, and he wasn't nor ever had been married. "Solid as a rock," BS assured us after we met him.

"A nice man," LC said not seeming overly concerned.

BS and Isiah quickly fell into a routine. A phone call on Wednesday night, a dinner date on Friday, Saturday afternoon at the movies, popcorn and TV that evening, and church on Sunday, the Presbyterian Church on 11th Street. BS seemed to glow. "I may begin baking those chocolate cakes," she smiled. Sometimes, LC went on those dates with the couple. All three seemed content in the relationship. After several months of dating, Isiah asked BS to meet his family for Sunday dinner. She came home telling us how warm and friendly his family had been.

"I'm happy for her and all," I said, "but it seems so boring."

"Everybody is so nice," Dorie said. "I mean so far there's no crazy grandmother, no drunken uncle, no unwed sister. Everybody has a job which they like. They get up every weekday and put on that uniform. Don't even have to wonder what to wear. There's no wild parties. Isiah always calls, always is dependable, isn't afraid at all. Why don't we meet men like that?"

"Because we're not BS," I said. "Think about it. If we met a nice boy like Isiah, would we give him the time of day?"

"No, he's too plain with that sandy hair and weak blue eyes."

"He does have a nice smile," I added.

"Yeah, and he's very clean," Dorie added. "He smells like soap."

"But to us, he's dull. A nice dull guy. We want some passion, some spark, some adventure!"

"Yes, and look where it gets us," I said.

"Maybe that's part of the problem," Dorie mused. "Maybe that's part of the adolescent fantasy that we hold onto, the knight on the white horse, sweeping us away. I don't think that BS even thinks about that. She likes the fact that he's ordinary and dependable and devoted to her in a quiet way. They are like a team of steady, big work horses, plodding through the furrows together."

"Yeah, and with LC as the frolicsome little colt, dancing around the plow." We laughed at the image, but it just about said it all.

The next thing we knew BS, Isiah, LC, and BS's family were invited up to Marysville for a Sunday dinner, and that seemed to put the final cement on the relationship. Isiah gave BS a lovely engagement ring, not too ostentatious, on Valentine's Day. And then the families began to plan for a June wedding.

JAMES

Out of the north country rode James. He ended up on our front porch pounding on the door.

"Ya wanna bag of beans? Rice?" he offered, when Dorie opened the door.

What on earth!

Dorie had married James some twenty years previously. It had been a temptuous marriage from the beginning. James was a womanizer, an egotist, but a guy that worked hard and made money remodeling one house after another and selling them for a profit. He came from a long line of abusers, and he saw his mission in life to keep his wife "in line" with verbal abuse and threatened physical abuse.

After the divorce, the son of a bitch had never paid child support. He had never visited his child or maintained a relationship with her. But under the circumstances, that was fine with Dorie. She wanted nothing except distance between them. But here he was again.

"Been down to the co-op buying beans and rice," he said.

"Beans and rice?" Dorie stammered. "No, I don't want beans or rice or you standing in my doorway. Now, go away!"

"Aw, come on, Dorie. Make me a cup of coffee and let's talk for awhile. A man gets lonely."

"Are you kidding?" she said in exasperation. "No talking, never again. Get out!"

"You never could be human and just give me another chance," he said.

"Give you a chance? Porn King? The baby sitter molester? You should be in jail rather than coming through my door asking me if I want a bag of beans!"

James glared at her and headed toward his truck.

"Someday you're going to regret this," he said over his shoulder.

"Never!" she yelled after him

We watched him drive away.

"What's his motive?" I asked.

"I have no idea," Dorie said tiredly, sinking down into the rocking chair. "But he's been following me around ever since I divorced him. Just pops up from time to time. Gives me the creeps as if he's watching me all the time."

"He never even asked about Chloe." I said.

"You noticed," she said sardonically. "He has no interest in Chloe except as perhaps a sex toy. Runs in the family. Evidently, his father was known for his predilection for underage girls. My sister-in-law told me that at the time of my divorce. Like father, like son," she had said. Just gives me the creeps."

"You know all those veiled warnings that our mothers gave us about men," I mused. "We understand in now, but we really didn't as children, young girls. We knew that there was something ominous about men, that we were told to stay away from them. I wonder what the generations of women in our families experienced, endured, what they wanted to keep their daughters safe from?"

"My ex-counselor friend told me that incest is just a part of normal family life in some communities," Dorie said, "told me there's one school district in the north area where the counselors hear about it all the time but not as a complaint, just a fact of family life. They don't even report it."

"Report it?" I asked. "Are counselors supposed to report it? To whom? Under what circumstances?"

"I'm not sure, but she told me that there are laws on the books now that say a counselor, doctor, social worker… all of them are supposed to report sexual child abuse to the police. It is a crime. But there's still this reluctance to do so. There's still this idea that what happens in a family stays in the family. Or people don't want to get involved in this stuff, too much shame attached."

"You think Chloe's Dad's attitude has anything to do with her behavior now? All this running from one group to another. All this lying and stealing. All these weird friends. From what you say, she was never like that as a child up until a few years after the divorce when she hit sixteen or so. Could trouble have been brewing down deep inside ever since? Did her Dad ever hurt her?"

"I don't know," Dorie said, "but there sure doesn't seem to be any way for me to help her now. She's as reluctant to get into counseling the last time she was here as she ever was."

"Yeah, sure, counseling," I said grimly. "Remember what happened to us? What would it be like for Chloe to go into counseling for incest and get seduced again? Who can you trust in that world, anyway? And that makes me think that…O.K. you have this law about reporting sexual abuse…then you have a counselor that seduces his patients. Is he going to open his mouth? I don't think so."

I poured us two sherries, sat down on the couch across from the rocking chair, and we talked into the night about the whole issue, frequently stopping to mimic "you wanna bag of beans?" for comic relief.

𝒦

KITCHEN

K stands for kitchen, that special place in every house where people gather and cook meals. We both loved to cook so there was no problem about that; we decided that we would take turns. Dorie would cook one week and I would the next. We would surprise each other with delicious little repasts. I really looked forward to the week that Dorie cooked. Her energy and imagination created some superb dishes. I remember some random man at our dinner table saying, "Do you girls eat like this all the time?" We broiled fish, made fruit slaws, Chinese casseroles and Irish stews. Our tossed salads and barbecued chicken were wonderful to behold.

Eating was a special ritual in our house. We came home to a glass of wine and a few pieces of Swiss cheese. One of us prepared our meal. We finished off with strong coffee. We always had a "little something" for dessert, a piece of See's candy, a snickerdoodle cookie.

However, there were those nights when we'd come home and decide to go out to eat. Friday nights we went to Capitol Tamale, but there were some Wednesdays or Tuesdays when we'd had a hard day and just had no inclination to cook. We would argue that it wasn't our traditional night to go out, that we really shouldn't spend the money, but in the end, out we'd go. We really didn't want a big meal or an expensive meal, nothing too starchy, just good, well prepared little meals. Now where should we go?

Pancake Parade was too noisy, and besides you had to beg for more than one cup of coffee. Lyons was too far a drive out to Country Club Center. Drive-ins were out of the question. Eppies was too expensive for what you got. That little Chinese diner was closed on Tuesday. Sambo's was too limited. Luis's had great Mexican food, but all those beans and all that cheesy rice! By the time we got through our list of possibilities, we'd be starving and would usually end up at Pancake Parade because it was the closest.

We'd open the menu. Damn! Why couldn't you buy a little broiled fish, a crisp green salad. Oh no. The fish was breaded, fried, and came with mounds of greasy French fries. The waitress would stand on one foot and the other wishing to God that we'd make up our minds about our order. We'd ask for coffee and tell her we'd take a few more minutes to decide.

Just think of the kind of little restaurant we could run. We made lists of interesting menu choices on one of the napkins. Or maybe instead of a restaurant, we'd open a teashop. Yes, a teashop all pink and white with a wide selection of teas, and little frosted cakes. Cucumber sandwiches, or tomato.

Meanwhile the waitress would come back several times and begin to fume at our questions and inability to make up our minds. Finally, we'd make a decision, eat and leave, chiding ourselves for not staying home and cooking instead of hogging down pancakes and eggs at that vile place. Never again, we'd say. But another week would go by, and another heavy work day would bow us down, and we'd find ourselves back at the Pancake Parade discussing why we were there in the first place one more time.

"I suppose that you don't have a shrimp salad," I'd ask the waitress.

"This is a pancake house," she'd say, glaring at me.

"Yes, a pancake house," I'd concede. "Well, then how about a short stack, scrambled eggs on the side."

"Make that two," Dorie would say. "And, oh yes, we'd like to split an order of bacon."

The waitress would trundle away, we'd sigh with defeat, and then gobble every morsel in sight once the plated arrived.

LILIES OF THE FIELD

Consider the lilies of the field-

Neither do they toil nor spin...

Someone referred to us as "lilies," a derogatory word for lesbians at the time. People wondered about our relationship. I'm not sure why. But after we heard the word, Dorie quoted the biblical verse, and it became a big joke between us. We certainly weren't 'lilies' in any sense of the word because we toiled and spun constantly.

We had so many projects and interests besides our jobs and master degree classes. People were so curious about us. They couldn't pigeonhole us at all. If women could bake bread, they certainly count not write intellectual essays. It they were adept at sewing everything from their clothes to the drapes, they must be incapable of doing scholarly work on Henry James, they must not read Dorothy Parker or John Steinbeck. But there we were doing all of those things.

While we cooked, we discussed the imagery in William Blake's poetry. While we dusted the book shelves, we wondered about the Irish writer Lord Dunsany's concept of the soul. While we potted geraniums, we debated

Hemingway's description of women. And we endlessly discussed men and out jobs.

Dorie taught basic writing classes like English 1A at Sacramento State as a part-timer. I taught junior high at James Rutter School in the Elk Grove District, a Sacramento suburb. Dorie agonized every semester about whether she'd have a job. Mine was secure. I had health insurance and a retirement plan, but it was so awful at times that I could hardly stand it. The first semester we lived together, the department chairman at the college decided to divvy up the part time jobs among ten graduate students, giving each of them two classes rather than the three or four they requested.

"It's fair," he said.

"It's fair alright," Dorie quipped. "Now none of us have enough salary to live on!"

But the chairman said he felt like Solomon in making his decision. So, Dorie began looking for additional work. And she found it when she interviewed for the position of Preceptress in one of the girls' dormitories. She would get one thousand dollars each month plus board and room and benefits. She would have to move into the dorm, of course, and that would upset our plans to share H Street, but we discussed that one had to do what one had to do. The Dean who interviewed Dorie told her she had the job, and he would arrange a contract for her to sign the next day.

So, Dorie went over to the English Department and resigned from her part time job.

"You sure about this?" the chairman said. "You're one of our best."

"Well, if I am one of your best, why can't you give me enough work so that I can support myself? She asked.

"Oh, I have to be fair," he told her.

That night we celebrated at Capital Tamale and discussed what we should do about H Street. The thing was that Dorie had weekends, holidays, semester breaks, and the long summer break off. Wouldn't it make sense to keep paying a share of H Street so that she could live there during these times? Or should she just hole up in her dorm room during these breaks with no girls to supervise? We decided to figure things out after she signed her contract, which would spell her obligations out more clearly.

"Well, at least if Chloe shows up, she won't be able to move in with me even if she is just pass'en through," Dorie said.

"Yeah, and James won't be able to burst through the door asking you if you want a bag of beans," I countered.

The next day, Dorie took off at nine for her contract signing appointment, and I left for the hallowed halls of James Rutter. But when I came home, I found her sitting in the rocking chair crying.

"What is it?" I asked.

"They gave the job to somebody else," she said.

"But they told you to come sign a contract. They said that you were hired," I reasoned. "What happened?"

"I don't know," Dorie said, wiping her eyes with a Kleenex. "I got there and the Dean came in and said they decided to award the job to somebody else. There was no explanation except that he said he was sorry there'd been a mistake. I walked over to the English Department and talked to the chairman about putting me back in my teaching schedule, and he said he'd do it. He hadn't assigned the classes to anyone else yet. I'm lucky there. I could be sitting here with no job at all, but damn, I had my hopes so high. Now I better begin looking for more part time work somewhere."

I felt really badly for her. The next day I bought her a Raggedy Ann for comfort's sake.

Sometimes I felt guilty for having a full time job with benefits. Dorie's college job seemed much more intellectual and glamorous. She could discuss great ideas and forms of writing. All I could do was baby-sit two hundred and fifteen seventh graders a day, most of whom didn't give a rat's ass about learning anything. And the school district didn't have curriculum guides nor did they give us new teachers any training in what we were supposed to do. There were no textbooks or supplies. If it hadn't been for Carolyn showing me how to take an old 1940's textbook and type up its chapters in packets for kids to work through, I would have lost my mind. I figured that I couldn't go wrong teaching English if I taught them about capitalization, punctuation, and grammar. After working those packets, I read to my students, junior high novels that had won the Newberry Award or at least were mentioned favorably in The Hornbook, the quarterly children's literature bible.

A nice champion-teacher named Ralph showed a lot of movies and that took up the slack. I never had the department head or the principal ask me what I was doing. No one visited my classroom. As long as the students were relatively quiet, I was left alone. But I often asked Dorie what was the point of what I was doing?

We applied for community college jobs. Dorie was turned down even though she had placed well during the interview. I didn't make it to first base. The first interview was before a panel of seven men who leered at my legs and asked what I was doing at the present time. When I said I was teaching seventh grade, they snorted and just about ended the interview. Evidently, if I was a seventh grade teacher, I had no possibility of becoming a college level teacher in their minds. That was about the time that Dorie, having almost finished her master's, decided to apply at the University of California, Davis campus in the doctoral program. I thought about it, too. Dorie was accepted. I was not. Even though on paper, I had all the right grades and letters of recommendation, I received a letter from the university saying that the people in the English Department didn't think I was "PhD material." Now, what did that mean? When I read the letter, Dorie handed me Raggedy Ann. She had become a solace symbol between us.

Dorie picked up typing jobs, continued her part time teaching, and I signed on for another year at James Rutter. Dorie prepared for Davis in the fall, and I made more grammar packets. I envied Dorie, and she envied me in a gentle way.

"Well, you have a full time job," she'd say.

"Well, you have a job where you use your brain," I'd say back.

"Yeah, but I hardly have any money to live on," she'd say.

"Hm! At least you don't have to spend your day babysitting thirteen year olds," I'd remind her.

And then I'd remind her that I was reading Maria Rilke the other day and in his advice to a younger poet, he'd said, "Read constantly." And she'd wonder what Emily Dickenson had read as a child? And there we'd go toiling and spinning, curious about everything, and trying to define our terms, as Dr. Simon North used to suggest. No, we were definitely not lilies of the fields! who neither toiled nor spun.

$\mathcal{M}$

MOVING DAY...OR NOT

I had moved five times in two years before settling down on H Street. Dorie had moved three times. The thought of another move filled both of us with dread. Divorces, salaries and circumstances had caused our moves. Now, we settled down in our new nest like chickens in the henhouse straw. Nobody was going to force us to move again!

But we hadn't been on H Street over a month, when a determined knock came on the door. We opened it to find the landlord, Mr. Gentry standing there, leaning on a cane. Behind him was a bull dozer of a woman named Evelyn. Mr. Gentry looked frail and yellow as he listed to one side.

"We're here to inspect the property," Evelyn declared.

"But you just inspected it last spring before we moved in," Dorie reminded Mr. Gentry.

"Ah yes," he said, "but this here's Evelyn Lynch and she's the new property manager. I just can't get around much these days." Evelyn squinted her eyes at us.

"Don't landlords give their tenants a call, set up appointment times. Do they just burst through the door?" I asked angrily.

"We don't have time for phone calls. He's sick, you know," Evelyn jerked her head toward Mr. Gentry, who now sat down in one of our dining room chairs. Evelyn began to inspect the kitchen, pulling our drawers and looking into the oven and refrigerator.

"Hm. Cracked linoleum," she muttered, looking down at the floor.

"Evelyn, look at that back porch, will you?" Mr. Gentry asked. "It's not in good shape."

Evelyn didn't answer but headed up the stairs to go through our bedrooms.

"There's an awful crack in the kitchen ceiling, and it seems to be bulging downward. I hope the tub above it doesn't come crashing through one of these days," I said, smiling at Dorie.

"And the eave spouts," Dorie added. "They're falling away from the building, and they're all clogged up anyway. They need to be cleaned out."

Mr. Gentry looked down at his shoes.

"Well, that about does it," Evelyn declared, coming back down the stairs. "We'll be leaving now."

She helped Mr. Gentry to his feet, and they departed through the front door.

"She never looked at the back porch," Dorie said.

"Nor the crack in the kitchen ceiling," I said.

About a week later, the phone rang one Saturday morning. It was Evelyn. Dorie listened for a few minutes and then began to sputter. "But that doesn't make sense," she said before hanging up.

"That battle ax!" she declared. "She is going to increase our rent by fifty dollars to raise money for all the repairs that need to be done. Damn. I knew that we should have insisted on a lease rather than just rent month to month."

"I know, but we were so gun-shy, after all the circumstances of our moves…" I trailed off.

"Well, we could pack our boxes and just move someplace else," Dorie suggested, but both of us drooped at the thought of it. And where would we go that would be the right size and so convenient? And by the time you counted the cost of a move, you might just as well stay where you were and pay the additional rent. We agreed.

A few days later, Dorie went out on the back porch to take the garbage out when the rotten wooden plank floor gave way, and down she went right through it, scratching up her right leg badly. I rescued her, helped her to the bathroom, where we bathed her leg, and put iodine on her cuts. It didn't appear that she needed medical attention. But the leg hurt like hell. She hobbled downstairs and sat on the couch with her leg elevated. I made up an ice pack for it. And then I got on the phone.

"Mr. Gentry, this is Cat on H Street," I began. "My friend, Dorie, just fell through the floor of the back porch. The rotten wood gave way. No, nothing is broken, but she's scratched and bruised badly. Do you have any insurance, liability insurance, I mean?"

"Oh, you'll have to talk to Evelyn about that," he said.

"What's her number?" I asked

I could hear him fumbling around. Eventually, his voice came back on the line.

" I can't find her number," he said.

"Well, look, Mr. Gentry," I said. "My friend's leg is a mess. We need to be compensated for that, and the back porch needs to be repaired. We need to talk to Evelyn!" At this point he hung up on me.

"Son of a bitch." I ground my teeth. I called back, but no one picked up the phone. It rang about twenty-five times.

Dorie went upstairs to soak her leg in a bath, and I went to my typewriter to flip off a letter to Mr. Gentry when there was a knock on the door. When I opened it, Evelyn barged in.

"Got a call from Gentry," she said. "Where's your girlfriend? Let's take a look at the back porch. Geeze, that's a mess," she said, looking out the back door. "Where's what's-her-name?"

"She's soaking her damaged leg in the bath," I said. Evelyn glared at me and headed for the stairs.

"You can't go up there," I yelled at her, but she took the stairs two leaps at a time, and pushed open the bathroom door before I could reach her. Dorie yelped and covered her chest with her arms. Evelyn bent over and surveyed her leg, and then she hightailed it back down the stairs and out the front door. I handed Dorie a towel, and we just stared at each other, floored.

The next day Dorie couldn't go to work, could hardly walk, took aspirin and sat with her swollen leg up on a chair all day. I hated to leave her to go to work, but she told me she'd be fine. We put the phone right beside her, and I called to check on her during my coffee break at ten.

"You won't believe who I have just talked to," she said.

"Who? I asked.

"That awful Evelyn. She said they would have to raise the rent again in order to fix the back porch. There will not be compensation for me for pain, suffering, or time off work." I was just furious. We'd see about that!

That night we composed a letter to Mr. Gentry telling him that we would not pay additional rent, that you expected a month's free rent for your ruined leg, and if we didn't get what we requested we'd call the Better Business Bureau, the Housing Authority, our family lawyer! This was war!

We never received an answer to our letter. When the rent was due the first of the month, we subtracted Dorie's share with a reminder about why the sum was less. Mr. Gentry didn't answer his phone. Another month went by. Nobody showed up to repair the back porch. But finally, a man appeared at our door. He was a pudgy man in a business suit.

"Fitzsimmons here," he announced. "I'm your new landlord."

What?" we chirped.

"Oh, Mr. Gentry, the previous owner, died several weeks ago, and I've purchased the property."

"Oh," we said, introducing ourselves. "Is Evelyn still the property manager?" we asked in unison.

"Oh no," he said. "I'll handle that. Let's see, there is the matter of a caved in back porch, is that right?"

"Yes," we said, showing him the back door.

"Well, yes," he said. "I'll have Bob come by tomorrow and get this repaired. And, I understand that your leg was injured," he said, turning to Ann. "How's the leg doing?"

"It's fine, now," she responded.

"That's good. Quite good," he said, looking around at the downstairs.

"Mind if I go upstairs?" he asked. We nodded and he went up the stairs. We looked at each other with raised eyebrows. He came back down. "Seems to be in good shape. You've made a nice little home here," he said smiling. "Well, I'll be on my way," and with that he left. "Oh, by the way, here's my card with my address and phone number. Please send your rent to this address from now on. On the first? Is that the agreement?"

We stood there nodding like children.

"Gosh," I said, "maybe things will be better with this guy, and we won't have to think about moving."

"We can only hope," Dorie said.

A short time later, the phone rang. It was BS. "Hey, did a guy named Fitzsimmons look at your place?" she asked. "Says he's the new property owner?"

"Yeah, did he come by your place too?" I asked.

"Sure did. Looked everything over. Seems like a nice, reasonable man. Nothing could be as bad as that Evelyn-one."

"You can say that again," I laughed.

"Probably doesn't matter too much, though, since I'll be gone by June. Isiah and me, well, we're looking for a house. He says we need to invest in a real home and not just live in apartments."

"Where are you looking?" I asked.

"Oh, Isiah wants to buy a house in Arden Park. He says it's a nice neighborhood, well established, and we wouldn't have to put in landscaping or trees like you have to in a new subdivision. The houses are ordinary, but the yards are huge. We're looking at two that are up for sale this weekend."

"Sounds like a good plan," I said. "So, what will LC do when you get married?"

"Oh, we've discussed that," BS said. "Once we get the house, we're going to add a mother-in-law's apartment to it for LC. She's family. We want her right with us."

I got off the phone and related the news to Dorie. She looked somewhat mystified. "You don't suppose they have a ménage a trois going do you? she asked.

"Dorie McKenzie! How could you suggest such a thing?" I said astonished. I'd never thought of that even being a possibility, not with honest, ole BS and Isiah. And we broke down in giggles.

Nightmares and Other Dreams

I slept. My mind dreamed.

My mother stood over me. She changed into a she-demon, larger than life who smiled at me and beckoned me back into the moist, pulsing womb. The afterbirth had never been exuded from her body. My birth had not been finalized. She wanted to reclaim her fetus, and all of a sudden, I was sucked back into the pink, contracting slime, and I was in darkness and calm once more.

I floated and saw my father crouched in extreme fright at the edge of a vast ravine. It was filled with twitching, naked bodies. Arms and legs extended and fell, lolled, and flailed with helplessness. My father was terrified, yet fascinated. He couldn't move. He looked at me. "Just look at those people down there," he said.

Another night, another dream. I saw my Joe sitting on a high, grey metal stool at Andy's Tavern in Kilkenny. He laughed and his voice was soft as he began to play a soft ballad on his guitar and sing "If I was a carpenter, and you were a lady."

I twisted and turned in my sleep, awakened, and lapsed back into dream. Simon was sending me down a road which had bodies caught in fallen electric wires. I couldn't get my car down the road without running over those bodies. I got out of the car and tried to walk down the road stepping over the bodies, but they reached for me and tore at my clothes.

Another night. I was on a bus with movie stars and important people. The bus was very old. We were driving down the steep streets of San Francisco, and we didn't know if the brakes would hold. Everyone was frightened except me. I watched people outside as the bus whooshed by. Then our bus seats turned into airplane seats, and we were strapped in as if for take-off. A big machine came out of the ceiling of the plane. It encircled my head. It was going to crush me. Everyone around me began laughing.

Night after night, I had these dreams. I would awake, fear gripping me, sometimes my mouth would open to scream, but no sound came out. It would take a long time to go back to sleep.

One of the reoccurring dreams was about a family picnic at a park in Humboldt, Iowa. A river ran through the park, and I was about eight years old. I was playing near the water's edge with some cousins, when a beautiful music box floated past me. I began following it along the river bank watching it bob in the current. I wanted that music box, but try as I might, I couldn't catch it. But I heard the music coming form the box, and I remembered the tune when I woke up; it was nothing that I ever remembered hearing.

I began to keep a dream journal at Dorie's insistence. I began to read everything that I could find about dream analysis. What fears and insecurities were hidden in the unconscious mind? I began to wonder if I was going crazy. What was going crazy like, anyway? Were crazy people sleep deprived because they couldn't face the terrible dreams that would come upon them? Perhaps going crazy happened when waking reality and dreaming intensity joined together and couldn't be separated.

One morning after an especially frightening dream, I cried all through breakfast. I just couldn't face the world. So, I called in sick and since Dorie didn't teach that day, we sat about in our nightgowns discussing dreams for most of the morning. I read from my journal, and she read from hers. Dorie's dreams seemed to be predominantly that she was in an old hotel and couldn't find her room, or she stood upon the ridge of a cliff looking into the abyss and saw loved ones down in the valley. Many times an enormous white wooly mammoth came to her in dreams, docile as an old cat.

"What do you make of that one, dear Dr. Freud?" she asked.

"I have no idea," I answered.

Yet it felt good to be talking about our dreams, comparing them to the symbols in the Dream Dictionary that I had purchased, trying to figure out what was going on in our waking lives that appeared symbolically in our dreams. My tension began to wane.

"Hey, let's go to Tiburon, sit on the deck of the Chantilly, and drink wine," I suggested.

"You're on," Dorie said, and both of us hurried up the stairs to get dressed. That's what we needed. The sea air, the view from the Chantilly of San Francisco Bay, a glass of wine. Those three elements would surely chase our nightmares away!

O

ORTHODOXY

Dorie and I had been raised in Christian fundamentalist churches. We spent our childhoods memorizing Bible verses, singing the old gospel songs, listening to preachers for hours on end. We had learned to tithe and conduct prayers. Our mothers and grandmothers were proud of us, for in our families, this was a woman's world. Our fathers and grandfathers never went to church, and the women in our families reviled them for it. Our fathers were going to hell, we were told. They were unrepentant sinners in the hand of an angry God, and they would be punished.

It was all very confusing for a child. We saw our fathers as reasonable, hard-working, honest men who did their best by their families. Their only sin in our eyes was that they didn't go to church with our mothers. Would God kill them for this?

Our religious beliefs were dualistic. God and the Devil. Heaven and Hell. Our churches weren't mainstream. They were isolated and defensive. They had come out of the Great Awakening of the American 19th century. They were based on the interpretation of the King James Bible (no other version) by a "spontaneous" person who did not study theology, but who had a personal revelation directly from God. There was one thing about which these preachers were sure, and that was the Catholicism was the enemy. The European 15th century Reformation was still being fought by our churches. The Catholic Church was the whore of Babylon described in Revelation, the last book of the New Testament. And that was that.

So, of course, the more the preachers railed about the Catholic church, the more interested in it I became. I loved the old Bing Crosby/Ingrid Bergman movies such as The Bells of St. Mary's. When I was in junior high school, I had a group of Catholic friends, girls who lived in the neighborhood and went to Catholic school. They did quaint things like writing the names of the holy family on all of their homework assignments. At the top of the page, Mary was on the left, Joseph on the right, and Jesus Christ in the center. They went to daily Mass, even getting up at six a.m. one cold winter morning when a group of us had had a slumber party so that they could put their coats and boots over their pajamas and slippers and trundle off to church. It was all very exotic.

Eventually, my church seemed inaccurate, wrong, misguided, and anti-intellectual. As I became educated at American River College, reading history and literature, I had to study the religious beliefs and history of Europe. The more I learned, the further I moved away from the church of my childhood. Dorie, basically, had gone through the same experience.

And so, here was another great change in our individual cultures. Our mother's churches weren't ours. We rejected them, but just as sexual mores were confusing, so was obtaining new spiritual belief systems. Where did we go for enlightenment? One day I found St. Francis of Assisi, and with him, an answer to my spiritual questions. It all happened in a literature class where we were reading a survey of world literature. And there it was, his Peace Prayer and his

Brother Sun/Sister Moon prayer. Who was this poet-prayer maker? His story was intriguing, the son of a 13th century Italian fabric merchant, a rich, young troubadour, who gave up al of his material possessions to live the Gospel in the most simple of terms, a man who had a vast following down through the ages, religious and lay Franciscans. I had to find out more about them.

When I was sixteen, I had done a rebellious thing with my Mormon boyfriend. We had decided to go to a Catholic Church for Christmas Midnight Mass. We weren't particular about where we went. The church down by Sutter's Fort was the nearest to my boyfriend's home, and so that's where we went. Oh, the ritual, the orchestra music, the incense, the robes of the priests, the life size nativity scene to one side of the altar, and the mystical language…and all that getting up and down, and making the sign of the cross, and lining up for communion. It was wondrous to behold. I never quite got over it.

Now reading about St. Francis, I realized that the only Catholic church I had been in was a Franciscan one. Synchronicity.

And then I went to Ireland and decided to focus on Irish mythology, history, and literature. And then I went to Ireland and met Joe Byrne. And then I went to Ireland and became a Catholic. When I came home and moved in with Dorie, I found myself walking twelve blocks down to the Franciscan church on stuffy, dusty Sacramento fall days just to sit in the church and "say a few prayers" as Joe had taught me when we were together in Ireland. Joe always insisted in stopping at every church we came across although I don't think that he'd been to Mass on a Sunday in years.

And that was another thing about Catholicism; it seemed a balance between men and women. Men seemed to be as much a part of it as women; in fact, in some ways they dominated. Even those crowds of men standing around the outside of the churches in Ireland, smoking cigarettes, while their families were inside the church participating in the Mass, were acknowledging the importance of the ritual. They were there, if not inside.

"I think that I'm going to become a Catholic," I told Dorie one day.

"How are you going to break it to your family?" she asked.

"Well, maybe I don't have to," I countered. "My childhood church has already disfellowshipped me according to my mother; obviously I don't attend, and she doesn't know what I do in my daily life or on Sundays. We have a mutually agreed upon "freeze" on certain topics such as religion now. I could probably practice Catholicism for twenty years, and nobody would be the wiser." We laughed at that, but it was true.

The next Sunday, I began going to the 9:00 Mass at the Franciscan church, and it wasn't long before Dorie wanted to go with me to see what intrigued me so. "I got it," she said on our way to Pancake Parade after the ceremony.

"What? I asked.

"I got it!" she continued. "It isn't the religion that you're crazy about, it's that priest!"

"What priest?" I asked, stomach tightening because I knew that she was onto something.

"That handsome blonde priest that said the Mass today," she went on, "and don't you try to con me. I know that look on your face. I know what all that sighing means. You are lusting after that poor priest!"

"You can't have a love affair with a priest," I laughed.

"Oh, no?" she said, getting out of the car at the Pancake Parade.

We sat down, and she kept teasing me. "What's his name? Patrick? A good Irish name, at that. A lad from the ould sod. Wouldn't be surprised if his last name was Byrne," and she laughed at her own joke. We ordered coffee and a short stack. I frowned.

Several weeks later, after Mass Dorie insisted that we have coffee and donuts in the social hall. The thought terrified me. I wanted to be anonymous. I didn't want anyone asking me questions or being too friendly. This was probably a hangover from my childhood days where any stranger in church was waylaid as a potential convert. "Oh come on," Dorie quipped when I protested. "It's just a cup of coffee."

"But what if he's there? I said.

"Who? The Priest? Why wouldn't he be there? It's his church and congregation, isn't it? I would think he'd socialize after church just like everybody else." That scared me to death. What if he talked to me, asked my name? How could I talk to a priest? Oh sure, it was all right for Dorie. She talked to everybody. She talked to professors. She talked to the hoi polloi everywhere she went. But I didn't. I didn't know how.

"For a grown woman, a teacher, a girl whose been around the block, I just don't get where this shyness comes from," she questioned. "You can give a presentation to a master's degree class. You can stand up before a schoolroom full of ruffians and demand order, but you can't talk to a priest? If he says hello, you just answer back, that's all. Come on!" And she dragged me toward the social hall.

Dorie worked the crowd while I hunched in one corner trying to be invisible. Father Patrick sat in a circle of adoring, old women. I avoided looking at him. "Got the lowdown," Dorie said as we left the social hall.

"What lowdown?" I asked.

"About that priest. Don't you want to know? Everybody thinks he's the cat's meow, but he has a flaw. He drinks."

"What do you mean he drinks?" I asked.

"He drinks!" she said matter of factly. "He drinks too much. He's a lush."

"But he's a priest," I said in a shocked voice.

"Yeah, and the ministers in our childhood churches were righteous men that never slept with the young girls in the congregation," she said sarcastically. "I've told you the story about Julie Bond, that thirteen year old that got pregnant by that old reprobate, Elder Fogstyle. And then there was the time that young Pastor Hanson, the youth minister, was found with a group of naked boys having a circle...well, you know what I mean. Our mothers were always telling us never to be alone with the minister, but they never explained why. I just thought it was another one of God's rules or something."

"Well, if they were so afraid of sexual congress with the pastors of their churches, how did they reconcile that with their religious beliefs? And why in the light of those events were they so hard on our dads? It was downright abusive to turn us away from our dads over religion. Was it a real belief? Or a power play? Or was it just another thing that women had to put up with when it came to men? I just don't get it."

"Neither do I," Dorie said, "but back to the point. This guy drinks way too much and everybody knows it."

"I could go to that church for twenty years and never know a thing about the priests," I told her. "You go for two months, and you get the goods on them. How do you do it?"

"You just have to know how to ask questions," she said, "and then you listen real hard."

Fall turned to winter and the Christmas season. Dorie and I decorated the house and put up a tree. We made wassail by the gallon and frosted tree-shaped cookies. We secretly squirreled away little treats for each other's stockings. And after a Christmas eve dinner of baked turkey breasts and mashed potatoes, broccoli, salad and string bean casserole, we headed out on a frosty night for Midnight Mass. By this time, we were pretty good at following the Missal and figuring out what was going on during the ritual. We liked it. We felt uplifted. And then on this particular night, Father Patrick came down the aisle and sat on the altar. He was weeping. We could all see it. He kept pulling a handkerchief out of his brown robed sleeve and wiping his eyes and nose. When he got up to give the homily, his words were a bit slurred as he talked about the holy family's journey on this holiest of nights. "God love him," an old woman behind us said.

A few weeks passed. One evening I announced that the time had come. I was going to the friary beside the church to ask about admission to the church. I worked up the courage, and drove to the building after work the next day, got out of my car, walked up the front steps, and rang the bell. An old lady answered.

"Yes?" she said, eyeing me kindly.

"I would like to speak to a priest…or someone," I floundered "about becoming a member of this church, a Catholic, I mean."

"Surely," she said, opening the door wider and leading me through I into the hallway where she opened a door to the right. She ushered me into a small room. It had a few easy chairs and a small table on which a bouquet of flowers had been arranged. She shut the door, and I sat there wondering what was to come. I had to wait some time before Father Patrick himself entered the room. He looked closely

111

at me, shook my hand, and asked how he could be of help. I could tell he wanted to escape.

"Well, I've been thinking about becoming Catholic," I began, "but I don't know the procedures."

"Oh, well," he said. "That's easy. Just take this book home and read it through," he said, reaching for a fat book from the shelf. "If you have any questions, just call. Have you been baptized before into another church?"

"Yes," I said, "a fundamentalist church to which my family belonged, but I left it behind some time ago. I'm an English major, well, a teacher now with a master's degree, so you know we had to read European and English history, and that's where I got interested in Catholicism. It really began when I read the prayer of St. Francis in one of my classes. And then I began coming here, and altogether, I made my decision."

"Well, then you're probably ahead of the game," he said, handing me the New Amsterdam Catechism, all eight hundred pages of it. "Just read along, and let me know if you have any problems." He rushed out the door.

It took me a month to read the New Amsterdam Catechism. No, I didn't have any questions. Everything squared with what I already had studied. I understood the theology. That was that. I called the friary and asked for Father Patrick. When he came to the phone, I told him that I'd read the catechism, and now what was I supposed to do?

"You don't have to go through baptism since you've already done it. Baptism is baptism, no matter what church did the deed. But you will have to be confirmed. We do that Holy Saturday evening, the day before Easter Sunday. Call me the Friday before and remind me. You have to have a sponsor, and I'll find you one.

"Does it strike you that something is missing here?" I asked Dorie. "I'm not sure what. But this is all so business like. It's just like buying a used car or something."

"Maybe you scare him," she suggested.

"Scare him? Why would I scare him?"

"Why do you scare most of the guys that you meet?" It was a rhetorical question that we'd often discussed. We saw the reaction in their eyes, the interest, and then the fear. We referred to these guys as scared rabbits. "Maybe he's Peter Rabbit, himself!" she laughed.

"But he's a priest," I countered.

"Yep, and he's a man," she said. Well, I'd have to think about that one.

The night of Holy Saturday came. I dressed carefully and made my way to the church an hour early. I rang the bell at the friary door but nobody came to answer, so I went to the church to wait. I sat there alone wondering what on earth was supposed to happen, thinking about the decision upon which I was acting. Little by little, people began dribbling into the church. There was no sign of Father Patrick. Eventually, Dorie came up behind me. "What's happening?" she asked.

"I don't know," I said mystified.

The ceremony was supposed to begin at 7:00, and about five minutes to seven, in came Patrick with an entourage of people. Where had they been? Why hadn't I been invited to join them? Hurriedly, he motioned me to join them and introduced me to a very round thirty-year-old woman dressed in jeans and a T-shirt. "This here's Judy," Patrick said. "She's your sponsor."

"What exactly is a sponsor?" I whispered to Judy, but she just winked, got into the processional line, and said, "follow me." And so I did. And that is how I became a mime of sorts, went through the ceremony, received the body and blood of Christ, and was told "Now you're a Franciscan Catholic," as the procession wended its way out of the church. I felt confused.

We stood on the church steps, and Dorie came toward me to give me a hug. "Got all that catechism down?" she asked.

"Nobody asked me anything about it," I said out of the corner of my mouth.

"Going to the party?" Judy said, stepping toward me.

"What party?" I asked.

"Oh, Mrs. Mooney's party," she said. "She always gives a party after the Holy Saturday services. Just follow me. We'll walk. She lives just a few blocks away.

"A party?" I said to Dorie. "A party after taking solemn vows? I think that being a Catholic is going to be fun."

"Well, you have a good time," she said, turning to leave. "I've got a late date."

Mrs. Mooney lived in one of those big, old houses that lined I Street a few blocks away. When we got there, all the lights were on, rock music played loudly from the stereo, and a full bar was set up. People began pouring in, making themselves sandwiches from the cold cuts and breads on a sideboard, and pouring themselves drinks. People introduced themselves, patted me on the back, kissed me on the cheek, congratulated me on becoming a Catholic, and then Father Patrick came in, none the worse from wear, as the saying goes. I faded into a corner and lit a cigarette. He looked over at me, and headed for my corner. I expected some spiritual advise or perhaps a handshake as a new member of the congregation.

"Can I bum a smoke," he asked.

"Why, ah, sure," I stuttered. I held out the pack, and he took a cigarette, lighted up, and retreated into the living room. That was about the time the dancing began. Little kids danced with their grannies, teenagers danced alone, couples, old and young, danced with each other. People were having a very good time, and Patrick bummed another cigarette.

After awhile people began forming groups and telling hilarious parish stories, like the time that Edna fainted on the altar and rolled down the steps and ended up under the front pew. She was a large woman and when the paramedics came, they had a hard time unwedging her. Or the time that Father Philip, who was quite old, went to light the communion candles, dropped the lighter, and set the altar linens on fire. One story followed another. We laughed until our stomachs hurt, and Patrick continued to bum cigarettes.

I left the party at about 2:00 a.m. The heavy drinkers were still hard at it. I wondered how they'd ever make it to Easter services. "Hey, thanks for the smokes," Father Patrick yelled in my direction as I was walking thought the door.

"You're welcome," I waved back toward him.

The next morning we slept in. I came down the stairs for my coffee about 9:00. "Hey, aren't you supposed to be in church or something?" Ann asked.

"Yeah, it's Easter. I guess so," I said, sitting down at the t able with my coffee. "But I had enough church last night, and besides I'm all out of cigarettes."

"Huh?" Dorie said, squinting her eyes at me.

"It's a long story," I said.

P

PRICE

I sat in my living room in Fort Dodge, Iowa, two years after living on H Street with my friend Dorie. I opened Christmas cards, reading them enthusiastically. Here was one from Evor Price. "Hoped you might be coming to Sacramento for the holiday season. I miss you. I'm all out of girlfriends at the moment."

"Indeed," I thought.

I picked up a glass of wine, sipped a few mouthfuls, and sat back in my chair thinking of Evor Price. It had all begun in December of my year living on H Street when Simon North decided that I had been moping long enough over my Irishman, Joe Byrne. He invited me to the movies where Dr. Evor Price, a colleague and friend of his from the English department joined us. We saw some non-descript movie, and then went to a pub nearby to have a glass of wine and talk about the movie. We discussed it very academically, and then the subject of Dr. Price's divorce came up. We discussed that academically also.

Simon dropped me home, and Dorie and I talked about Dr. Price. He was about forty-five, tall, tanned from playing tennis every day, athletic, with grey hair, big grey eyes, and a very chiseled, handsome, Viking face. He was Norwegian, and had been raised in Iowa and Minneapolis. His father was the president of a Lutheran College, and all of his brothers were clergymen. Dorie thought him quite respectable, but neither of us had ever taken a class from him. The story went that his wife had run off with a tennis instructor. It seemed that she began taking lessons and that led to more than a good backhand.

"What's Simon up to?" I questioned.

"I think this evening was a set-up for you both," Dorie concluded. "You just wait. Price is going to call and ask you out."

And that's exactly what happened a few days later.

"Hey, Cat," he began, "what are you doing New Year's Eve? I'm invited to a party at Fred Lawson's. Pick you up at seven if you'd like to go."

"Sure," I said. "Sounds like fun." I got off the phone and panicked. What on earth was I going to wear? What should I do with my long blonde hair that hung down my back? Jewelry? Oh dear God! What jewelry would I wear? And Fred Lawson? He was another English teacher at the college, middle-aged, somewhat boring from what I had heard. There would probably be English Department people all over the place. How would I act? What would they think when Price showed up with me?

"They're just folks," Dorie quipped as I colored the air with questions. "You'll probably find them terribly boring."

"What are you doing New Year's Eve?" I asked. "I wish Simon would ask you out to the same party so I could have some backup."

"Well, Simon never goes to parties that I know of," she said, "and this year I've decided to stay home and read a good book. I'm sick of New Year's Eve parties with a bunch of yahoos, or going out on Amateur Night with terrible service, doubled prices for food and drink, and people getting drunk all over the place. Oh no, I'm through with that scene. I'm going to be sitting here in my jammies with a good book as a companion. Most sensible thing I've ever done."

"All of a sudden it's sounding awful good to me," I said. "Perhaps I should cancel."

"No, I think that you should go," Dorie said. "If it's comfortable, and you like Dr Price, it might be a fun thing to pursue. Simon is right. You've moped around long enough."

The following Saturday, Dorie and I went to Joseph Magnin's to find something for me to wear. The long black dress? Too matronly and funereal. The short red cocktail dress? No, I'd look like a floozy. We pawed through racks of clothes. I went to the dressing room with armloads of things that weren't right, and then we found the perfect outfit. Long, sleek navy blue heavy knit pants with a tunic in cranberry, which slipped gracefully off the shoulders and hung to my knees. The tunic had navy trim. It was subdued but elegant. It cost a fortune, but it was worth every penny. Next we found a pair of crystal earrings, danglers that would look festive. And we decided that I'd wear my hair long, slightly curled at the edges, and pushed behind my ears, showing off the earrings.

The night of New Year's Eve, I spent an hour getting ready, being very careful with my makeup and hair. "You look great," Dorie told me as I came down the stairs. I was as nervous as a cat in a crowded room. And then the doorbell rang. Dorie answered it, and there stood Dr Price, looking like a movie star. He wore jeans, a white silk shirt, and a navy velvet blazer. He smiled, took my arm, and escorted me to his car. I could see Dorie watching us from the porch. She waved as he drove away to the suburbs to the house of Fred Lawson. We made polite conversation along the way.

The Lawson's lived in a posh neighborhood in a house that had started out as a three-bedroom rancher. But remodeling had added on rooms and patios and the house was a miniature Winchester Mystery House. The house had already filled with people and music played, glasses clinked, and the front door was wide open even though it was a foggy, cold night. "Come in, come in," someone yelled at us. Heads turned, and several men smirked. Oh I could tell what they were thinking. Well, so what if I was about seventeen years Dr. Price's junior. So what?

He introduced me to a few people. I recognized faces from the English Department. It was interesting to see these professors now with their wives in tow. What strange couples some of them made. Dr. Price seemed to enjoy showing me off. He left me standing alone to go into the family room and get us drinks. I just stood there smiling and nodding at people. Eventually he came back, motioned me to one side of the room where a few couples were gathered listening to a woman's laughter and stories. He seated me with them, and then he said he'd be right back. He wandered off into the crowd, and then he just disappeared.

I tried to listen to the deadly dull conversation. Dorie was right. And then Charles, a young gay man from the Department came over to ask me to dance. Thank God. I got out of that clique, I thought. On the way to the dance floor, a brash old woman brushed up against me. "Don't bother, honey," she said. "He's a fag." She blended into the crowd on the dance floor. I glared after her and saw her dancing by herself. Charles and I finished the dance, and he went to the bar while I drifted into another conversation group.

Dr. Whitford's wife was regaling the group with stories of the operating room in which she worked as a nurse. Her stories were filled with blood and gore and mistakes made during surgery and jokes the doctors played on each other. I found the stories quite horrifying. A few people in the group laughed, and her husband looked down into his drink glumly. He'd probably heard all this before.

A woman in a billowing blue chiffon dress hurried down a hall. I watched her from behind. I could have sworn that she was on the arm of someone wearing a navy velvet blazer. I smilingly nodded at the Whitfords and moved from the group over to the bar for a refill of my wine glass. Sidney, another acquaintance from the gay brigade as Simon called them, stepped up beside me. "How's things shaken?" he asked, looking over the crowd.

"Well, actually I'm rather bored," I told him, "and my date seems to have disappeared!"

"Oh, God," he said, looking over the room not much interested, cruising the place with his eyes.

"What are you up to these days?" I asked him.

"Not much. Just raising succulents and pugs," he replied, still not looking at me.

"Succulent plants and pug dogs," I said, "interesting combination."

"Huh?" he said, "Oh yes, I guess it is. Well, see you later. I see a friend over there."

He picked up his mug of beer and sauntered off. The bartender refilled my glass. Dr. Clyde came over. I knew him rather well. He had been the faculty sponsor when Dorie and I went to Ireland. It's a wonder that he still spoke to me after I had disgraced his group, running off with Joe. But he was as gentlemanly as ever.

"Want to dance?" he asked. He swept me off the stool and out onto the floor, and we began to dance when his wife approached with murder in her eye. She grabbed his arm and spun him around. At first, he was startled, and then he reddened and in a furious hiss said, "Donna, don't you ever do that gain!" Donna stood her ground, and Dr Clyde led me back to the bar, apologizing all the way. "Sorry about that," he said. "She's had too much to drink."

I listened in on the bar conversation, laughed at a few jokes, prowled around the room, and saw Price standing out on a patio with his arm around a young thing wearing gold lame pants. Then the woman in the blue chiffon caught him by the arm and waltzed him toward the open patio door where they disappeared. The party wore on, a woman wearing a black hooded dress sitting to one side of the bar began to laugh hysterically, a couple next to me got into a fight over some unintended slight, and I looked hopefully at the clock. It was almost midnight. Someone began a countdown. Ten, nine, eight…Happy New Year! Everyone around me was hugging and kissing, someone threw confetti up into the air and laughed uproariously as it rained down on our heads. People began tooting those awful little horns that the hosts had handed out half an hour before, and then, there he was…Price, grabbing me up into a hug, kissing me softly on the mouth, and murmuring in my ear. "Well, you're just the prettiest girl here. You just are!" He sounded like it annoyed him.

A wild rhythm came on the stereo and people began dancing with abandon. Price pulled me out onto the floor and twirled me around. "Hey." He shouted over the music. "Why don't you come home with me tonight?" A few people dancing near us turned to look at us. I smiled at him.

"Dr. Price, how you do go on," I said in a Southern accent. The music ended and a slow tune began. Price held me close and nuzzled my neck. Oh, spending the night with you would be delicious," he said.

"Really? Why didn't you spend the party with me?" I asked.

"I think it's time to go." Price backed up and stumbled away to find our coats, and I proceeded to the front door to wait for him. I tried to find the hosts to thank them for the party, but they were nowhere in sight. Price showed up and helped me on with my coat and we retreated into the cold night air. We got into the car and he started it reciting the prologue to the Canterbury Tales

"What are you doing?" I asked.

"Oh, I always recite the C.T. while the car warms up. It's an old Iowa winter habit," he said in all seriousness. He put the car into reverse, stepped on the gas, and we sprung backwards, crashing into a stonewall! "Heavens," he exclaimed, putting the car into drive as he narrowly missed a parked car as we roared down the driveway.

"Drive careful," I admonished him.. "You're scaring me." He ignored me, of course.

Neither of us said another thing on the way home. We got to H Street, and I slid from the car.

"Great party, thanks a whole bunch," I said, slamming the door behind me. He drove off.

"Well, that's the last I'll see of him," I thought.

Dorie had not waited up for me, which I wouldn't have expected. It was about one a.m. and I went to bed. The next morning over coffee I shared my story of the infamous New Year's Eve party with Dorie, and for the next two weeks that's all we talked about. Why had Price taken me to a party, ignored me all night, and then suggested that I go home with him? What was wrong with that picture? None of it made sense. We consulted Simon, but he was no help. And then the phone rang. It was Price suggesting that we have a beer at the Pine Cove.

We sat at the Pine Cove, sipping beers, amidst the blue cigarette smoke and never mentioned the party at all.

Every couple of evenings, Price would call with his Pine Cove invitation. And I would go, completing the ritual. Pick up, ordering a draft, talking about common gossip, politics, the weather, nothing personal, and a quick trip home, a kiss at the door, and Price rushing off, leaving me confused about the would be relationship.

The week after Easter, I flew to Iowa to visit my father. My stepmother drained the morning bacon on a newspaper from Fort Dodge, some sixteen miles away from my family home in Humboldt, and there right under the bacon grease was an ad for an English teacher at Fort Dodge Community College. I called, applied, asked for an interview before I flew back to California, got one, and within a week after getting home I received a call offering me the job.

I was thrilled and devastated at the same time. Thrilled to be given the career opportunity, devastated knowing that I'd have to break up my nest with Dorie. But somehow, we both had known that it was temporary such as the time that Dorie had applied for the job as dorm mother and would be living somewhere else most of the time.

We still had not accepted a relationship that would be central, that our living arrangements would be central, that our commitment to each other would be central. If she or I deemed to go off on an adventure with a job or a man, it was accepted by the other that that would come first. If a man moved into your life, even your best friend took second place. A job emerged that was a career step upward, well of course, you had to take it. And so I prepared to pack my things come June.

One late May evening as I sat among boxes sorting out books, a knock came on the door about eleven. There stood Price, roaring drunk. He'd been at the Pine Cove for hours. Dorie had already gone to bed, but I knew that voices from downstairs would probably awaken her. "Shsss." I shushed him when he came into the room and began to shout. But he was caught up in some madness. He began to pacing and ranting and raving about his ex-wife and how he would teach her a lesson. "Two could play at her game," he said as if it was an ultimatum. He began taking off his clothing and flinging items across the room. Off came the tie, then the shirt, and then he unzipped his pants. I sat in the rocker watching with fascination.

"You think that you can ruin everything, take away my children, and just begin a new life? What about all of our plans about building a new house?" I could hear Dorie hiccupping with laughter at the top of the stairs.

"Dr. Price," I said with as much dignity as I could muster, "you have to put your clothes back on and go home!"

"What?" he said, blinking at me. "My clothes? What do they matter when that bitch ran off with the first man available?"

"Please, Evor, you have to get dressed and go home," I giggled.

There he stood, this tall, tanned, handsome man in his underwear, fiercely frowning at me.

"Well, if that's the way you feel about it," he said haughtily. He began picking up his clothes and headed toward the door.

"You can't leave without wearing your pants," I said, stopping him at the door.

"Just watch me," he said, blinking. "I shall call again." And with that, he lurched out the door, walked to his car, and fumbled around trying to find his keys, probably in his pants' pockets. He slowly started the car and weaved down the street.

Dorie was downstairs before his taillights were gone. We collapsed on the couch together, laughing our heads off.

"Has that man lost his mind?" Dorie asked. "Now I've seen it all."

The next morning we were still laughing about the whole silly scene.

"I think that he really likes you," Dorie said, "but every time he thinks about it or feels too much, it scares the bejasus out of him, and he has to stay away for awhile to cool down. And then he has a hard day, gets drunk, and where does he head? Where does he feel safe to rant and rave? Taking his clothes off? I can't figure that one out at all. What could that be a symbol of? Stripping himself of this anger? What?"

"I think that you're on to something," I answered. "I really like him too, and I'll miss him. But somehow, I don't think I'll experience this kind of thing in Fort Dodge, Iowa."

"Oh, you never know," Dorie smiled at me over her coffee. "There's craziness everywhere these days."

2

QUIET BEFORE THE STORM

Even when things were going well with Dorie and I, our lives peaceful as can be, other people would impose on us bringing their troubles to our doorstep. For instance, there was the time that Dorie's sister called from Oregon to say that she and her husband were coming through town on their way to Mexico. They'd be at our place the next day, staying just long enough to say hello. Dorie rather winced at the call. There had been trouble before when these two had visited.

The next afternoon, they arrived. It was the first time that I'd met Janie, a slim, pretty, blue-eyed woman with long page-boy hair and Orville, a big, burly, dark haired biker type man. They came in with a six pack of beer and began to drink. Both chain smoked. It wasn't long before they were slurry with beer. Dorie suggested that they stay for dinner and went to the kitchen to whip up something. Janie and Orville began to argue about some vague thing.

At the dinner table, the argument escalated into a screeching yelling, name-calling fight. Dorie and I ate small bites, horrified at what was taking place before us. Before Dorie could pour the after dinner coffee, Orville stood up, gave his wife a parting shot, and slammed out the door taking off. He'd threw Janie's suitcase out of the car and onto the lawn where Dorie retrieved it.

What else could we do but take her in. She was quite drunk. She was crying. We couldn't trundle her down to the Greyhound station and send her packing. So began a week of mornings watching Janie drink copious cups of coffee, staring into space. About three, she began drinking beer, and by seven pm, she was wailing again. She was making no plans to leave.

On a Friday night, Dorie came in from work and found Janie rocking back and forth in our rocking chair, knitting furiously.

"Janie, you've got to get yourself together, make a plan, do something. It isn't helping the situation, you just sitting here as if Orville is going to appear at the door and everything will be all right."

"Well, big sister, it's your fault," she spat out.

"What?" Dorie reacted.

"You heard me. It's your fault, you and you high-faluting ways, always trying to put the make on Orville, wanting him for yourself."

"Janie, the last man on the face of the earth that I would want anything to do with would be Orville. In fact, I think that you should leave him. He's mean and he hurts you all of the time. You need to get away from him."

"Yeah, just as you got away from old James? That's always your solution, isn't it. You with your big, fat education, always throwing it in our faces. Why can't you just leave me alone." She began to sob.

I had sat passively, listening to this outrageous conversation. Then I couldn't help myself.

"Look!" I said to her. "You are the ones that invited yourselves here. You are the ones that started fighting. We tried to support you. We tried to make you comfortable this week. Dorie's education has nothing to do with anything, and as for flirting with Orville? Are you nuts? They hardly exchanged words the few hours that he was here. What is this shit anyway?" Dorie retreated into the kitchen and began rattling pots and pans.

"Well, if that's the way you feel about it, I'll leave," Janie yelled at me. I went to my room. There was no conversation down below. Within a short time, Dorie arrived and handed me a bowl of noodles and vegetables. "I'm taking her to the bus station early tomorrow," she said.

By the time that I got up the next morning, Janie was gone. Over coffee, I asked the question…"Why hadn't Dorie stood up for herself when her sister was being so mean?"

"Because she's my sister," Dorie said. "It's always been like that. When we were kids, she'd do something wrong, and I'd catch hell. She always blamed everything on me."

"Well, the time has come for you to fight back," I said. "Isn't there a time when you have the right to tell your family that you expect the same consideration out of them as you would of strangers?"

"You're right," she said, "I should not put up with her ever again. And you know what? By the time she gets to Medford, Orville will be home acting like nothing happened. Then their cycle of anger will start all over again. Why do I put up with her? Well, blood's thicker than water, I guess."

"Yeah, as my grandfather always said, 'you can choose your friends but not your relatives.'"

"Well, I won't have to see her until next Christmas anyway," Dorie grinned.

"You mean you're going to spend the holidays with that pack of ghouls?" I asked in amazement.

"If you don't come out from Iowa, I probably will get together for Christmas. It's tradition!" Dorie said.

R

REFRIGERATOR

Nobody gets stuck behind a refrigerator on a dusty, service porch. But that's where I found myself. I felt ridiculous. It had all begun when Dorie suggested that we move the old refrigerator from the service porch into the kitchen. Why was it on the porch in the first place? It wasn't convenient. It should have been a simple operation, but the big, old box was just too heavy for us to move easily. We shuffled and skittered the awkward old box toward the doorway. By the time we got it there, we understood why it was on the porch. It wouldn't fit through the doorway. With one final shove, we firmly wedged the thing into the doorjambs. It wouldn't go forward or backward. And the back door was in such a position close to the kitchen door, that the big old box jammed up against it too, making it impossible for me to get into the kitchen or out the back door. I was on one side and Dorie was on the other. We were separated by that silly, cold machine that froze the celery, but wouldn't make ice cubes.

"You could pass sandwiches over to me, and I could make the porch my home, I laughed. We both got the giggles. When we stopped laughing and caught our breath we decided that if we got the machine stuck, we could get it unstuck, but no amount of heave-ho made the refrigerator move. We huffed and puffed, we beat at it, and put our shoulders into the shoving, but nothing happened.

"Damn," Dorie said. "I'll have to call somebody to help us move this awful thing. I could hear her rummaging through the kitchen drawer where she kept her address/phone book. "We need a good strong man? she exclaimed.

"Yeah, where you gonna find one, never have before," I laughed. "What about Simon?"

"Oh he's got a bad back, goes to a chiropractor twice a week." I heard her go to the phone and dial a few numbers.

"Of course, nobody's home," she said, coming back into the kitchen.

"There's gotta be somebody around. Try some more," I suggested.

Dorie passed me a cup of coffee over the top of the refrigerator and went back to dialing numbers. I could hear wisps of conversation as I sat on the floor behind the refrigerator. Dorie came back into the kitchen.

"It seems that everybody has gone on vacation, is resting up from knee surgery, has a bad back like Simon, or has a car not running," she said.

With all those men banging on our door, chasing us around various office desks, leering at our legs, there wasn't one to be found when we really needed some help. "What about BS?" I asked, but BS and LC were at work.

"OK, I give up. How 'bout calling my ex. He could move anything. Here's the number," I said. Dorie stretched the phone cord as far as it would go, dialed the number, and handed the receiver up over the top of the refrigerator to me. "Are you sure you're up to this?" she asked.

I couldn't answer because Cal's voice sounded on the other end of the line. I told him what the problem was, and he sighed and said he'd be right over. In twenty minutes, he was there telling me what a dumb broad I was for getting into such a fix. Neither Dorie nor I argued particularly because we wanted that damn box moved. With one heavy lunge, the refrigerator gave ground, and within a few minutes, he had it walked right back to where it had begun. I came out from the corner of the service porch where I had been wedged.

"Thanks," I said icily.

He glared at us both, and left without another word. "Asshole," I muttered as I watched him drive away.

"Well, at least we got the refrigerator moved," Dorie commiserated. We had learned two things: (1) always measure your space before trying to move something into it; and (2) always measure your man by his usefulness in case of an emergency, even one like moving a refrigerator!

S

SIMON

I sat in Simon's class in literary criticism, a junior at Sacramento State University. He was elegant, and very intellectual, and terribly grand. I understood about every third word that he said in his lectures, but I couldn't wait to get back to the next one. Here was a man with something to say not only about literary criticism but about life and how it should be lived. He was a missionary, an extremely subtle missionary, but I caught on, and I lapped up his ideas as a cat laps a good bowl of cream.

Everyone tried to avoid his classes because he was known as a "prof that would really require you to work." Also, local gossip said that nobody got above a "C" in his class. Only the foolhardy or brilliant took classes from Simon. I had stumbled into it, definitely one of the foolhardy. I wrote a paper on Naturalism in literature as my final project. Indeed, I had gotten C's on the few things we had been evaluated on up to finals time.

I had to prove that I could think to this man for some reason. I sweated over the paper. I actually did research the way I was supposed to. I knew that I couldn't fake my way with him. And finally it was done, and I handed it in expecting another C, but feeling that this was really one of my best, honest efforts.

We had to go into his office to retrieve our papers, and he talked to each student that went through the door about his or her achievements in the class. When I approached him, he smiled very warmly and then said, "Cat, Oh yes, I remember your paper – you did a terrific job on this. You've got a good head on your shoulders, one of the few people that seems to be able to think on this campus." And with that he handed me the paper marked with an A-. "A few minor problems…I've discussed them inside." And he made a gesture with one hand.

"Thanks," was about all I could get out of my mouth. I left his office floating on air, shocked, surprised, elated. No one had ever told me that I was a "thinker" before. Me? A thinker. Could he have mixed me up with somebody else?

A year later, I signed up for a graduate class in Hemingway from Simon, and there was Dorie sitting right up in front as big as Huffy, as we said in the Midwest. Within a few weeks, we began reading our first papers to the class, and that's where the old Marine said stupid things and made me mad, that's where I wrote the note to Dorie who happened to be sitting beside me, and that's where the coffee date was extended to a lifetime of conversations.

And what did we find to talk about on that first coffee occasion? Simon, of course.

Simon! Simon's ideas, Simon's erudition, Simon's personality. Dorie knew more about him than I did, and she began sharing all the interesting things about his life. He had been instrumental in getting her into the graduate program, and had even arranged things so that she could teach a class for him in freshmen composition. He was proud of her, and had been her absolute mentor for several years. And on top of all that, she was in love with him. It was obvious.

The next day we met for coffee in the Faculty Dinning Room. I had never presumed to enter it. But Dorie was faculty and marched right in, ordered her coffee like nobody's business, and sat there like she owned the place. I followed suit. Simon joined us about ten minutes later, and said, "Well, I wondered when you two were going to get together."

"What do you mean?" I asked.

Well, you're just so damned alike. Sooner or later, you'd hook up. You're going to scare the bejasus out of people around here, you know?"

"I don't understand," I said.

"Come on, Si, what are you up to?" Dorie asked him.

"You just wait and see the reaction from people around here when they see the two of you with your heads together. One of you is forceful enough, but two of you will be a real threat."

Dorie rather nodded, Simon slurped coffee, and I didn't get it at all. But I soon saw what he meant. Many of the men around were leery of competent women, the gays didn't trust us at all, and other women were jealous since we were the competition. I began to realize how much I hated politics and being pigeonholed into a stereotype by people in the department. It was worse for Dorie since she went from graduate assistant to part-time instructor.

In everything I did from that time on, whether teaching a class of my own or writing a paper, I always did it with the ghost of Simon looking over my shoulder. Would he approve? How would he explain this fact? Would he be disappointed with my choice in this matter? And than I found that I explained what was going on in my personal life to Simon, in my own mind of course. Somehow talking out things with Simon, or the ghost of Simon lurking in my mentality, helped me to figure out what to do, or how to handle things. And the visible Simon always seemed to appear at the right time, such as the time he took me to the movie introducing me to Evor Price.

Simon had a very strange marriage; we'd never heard of anything like it. He shared his life with a wife in a beautiful, little cottage-style brick bungalow. I had flower boxes at the windows, a steep, black roof. He invited us over for a glass of wine one evening. His wife was away. Actually, she had an apartment in Los Angeles and spent a lot of time there. Husbands and wives that lived separately for months on end? It couldn't be true.

Inside, everything was elegant and perfect. Thick oriental rugs graced the hardwood floors. Art was perfectly balanced with heavy drapes, mullioned windows, window seats, and a comfy fireplace. We sat on the deep cushioned sofa drinking our wine and looking around at the finery. How could two people put together this lovely nest, but then live separately? And did they both engage in friendly and sexual liaisons with other people? Did they ever talk about it? Did they have some kind of strange agreement?

On occasion, when I was away, Simon spent the night with Dorie, lying on his right side after making love, always listening to his own heart. It was to be understood that he and his wife were together.

That was something very difficult for Dorie. First of all, it wasn't the pattern with which she grew up, and secondly, Dorie had "this thing" about a man and a woman and loyalty. Sleeping with someone meant commitment, and how could Si sleep with her or anyone else, and still have any emotion toward his wife? He tried to explain it. He tried to show Dorie that he and his wife were past those traditional patterns, those less than mature assumptions. They could love each other, and be best friends to each other, and then be off to their own world and interests. But this went against the very core of our upbringing, our basic beliefs about relationships.

We spent many fanciful hours trying to figure out how to lure Si into Dorie's snare. But none of our plans produced anything.

One day, Si sat drinking rum and grapefruit juice in our living room. We were discussing the metaphysical aspects of something or other when I realized that my mind had wandered. When I had brought it back to the reality of the conversation, I picked right up where I had left off. We were repeating the same things that we had said in a thousand other conversations. I hadn't seen that before. The realization rather shocked me. And there was something in that realization that I didn't want to think about. For if I thought about it, I would have to think about the fact that Si had intellectual limits, and that would lead to the idea that I perhaps had grown beyond what he had to offer. And if that was so, I would have to experience loneliness, and I would have to see that perhaps he was just a middle-aged man with feet of clay, a middle-aged man who could be boring. I did not want to have to deal with the fact that Simon might be boring because this would lead to another idea about mortality...someday, some bright eyed young upstart would also look at me and think, "She's drying up!"

So that I wouldn't have to think any of these thoughts, so that I could continue to worship Simon a bit longer, I excused myself from the conversation, and went for a walk.

$\mathcal{T}$
TURNING POINT

One of the great turning points in Dorie's life came when she applied for the full time position that opened in the English department. She wanted that job. But so did others, and it seemed that everyone who applied had not only an angle but a noisy group of supporters behind them. To make matters worse, the department chairman was a weak man who didn't like making decisions, and he didn't like fighting special interest groups. So instead of going through a search, an interview process, and hiring one of the candidates, he put the whole business off and scheduled part-timers into the vacant position. It seemed like there was no end in sight when it came to filling the position.

Every group that went to the chairman demanding action for their candidate only caused the paralyzation to grip the man more completely. Dorie didn't have a group behind her, but at the end of the semester, the Women's Caucus called to discuss the matter with her. "We've reviewed the situation," they informed her, "and you've got a good chance because all of the other candidates are men."

The next week the chairman saw a way out of the entire situation. He declared that he would only consider those applicants with PhDs. Nobody backed by the groups had one!

"Unfair," declared the Chinese-for-Academic-Freedom group. "The department hired a black last year with a master's degree only!"

"That right," agreed the Chicanos For Equal Rights in Hiring. The Women's Caucus agreed as did the Gays and the Free Speech Coalition and the Peace and Freedom political party. The issue couldn't be swept under the rug.

Dorie became an issue. The Women's Caucus argued over and around her, and the gays considered backing her after their candidate went off to a job in Washington State. (He had waited long enough, he said.) Si was campaigning for her, and the day eventually came when the department chairman announced that a panel of people representing all the elements involved in the political problem would be convened to interview the applicants. He figured that he could sluff the decision off onto the panel, and that it would take them so long to fight their way to any kind of agreement, that he would have a summer, or perhaps, a whole year of peace and quiet.

Dorie went to an interview. "Hello, Dorie, glad that you could come talk to us," a panel member said. And with that they were off and running. They argued one way and then the other. They pounded that table to emphasize their various points of view. They cited precedent. They read department history. And no one asked her anything or even included her in the tirade. After several hours, someone suggested that it was time for a drink, and they all left for the Fireroom, a famous off-campus dive where everyone of importance gathered to drink beer. "Oh, Dorie" someone said on his way out. "Thanks again for coming." The door shut, and there she sat at the big walnut conference table wondering what on earth had just happened.

The fight went on. It burned through the summer with panelists calling her almost every day to ask her opinion of one group or another's politics, and one night about 2:00 a.m., the phone rang and a Women's Caucus member hissed, "Don't give up Dorie, we knocked the nigger out of the race."

"Swell," she replied and went back to bed. It had started out as an interesting possibility, it had become a joke, and it was now becoming a nightmare. She had known from the start that nobody cared about her welfare, nobody cared how she would teach the classes assigned, nobody cared if she finished her PhD, and nobody cared what she thought. She was simply a pawn of the various groups pushing and shoving for recognition.

The thing wound down finally about the next November when someone insisted on a vote. I had moved to Iowa to begin a job at Ft. Dodge Community College. The panelists wrangled about the voting procedure for another month and finally a vote was taken. It came out seven to seven. It was a tie between Dorie and a Chinese man living here on a Visa from Hong Kong. He spoke almost no English. On the next vote, the gays came through strongly for her, and that tipped it. She was asked to join the faculty as a full time instructor.

She signed a contract and was invited to a celebration party. "I think that it's great you got the job and not Leroy Marvinstead," a tall black woman told her. "Of course everybody knows that you've been sleeping with Si for years in order to get it." And the woman minced away. She got the picture. This was a hollow victory as it had been a hollow fight. "What do you know about Chinese literature?" a student asked. "Do you think that you can bring anything new to it?"

"But I won't be assigned Chinese literature," Dorie answered him.

"Sure, you're not competent," the miserable little graduate student retorted, and got busy with his drink.

"Shit, all she knows is Henry James," someone said over the sound of the booze being poured over ice. And with that, Dorie calmly slipped out the door and headed for home. "I'm sure that they don't even know that I'm gone," she told me on the phone as I sat in my Iowa apartment.

And they didn't. Dorie slumped glumly around the house for a few days, and then began to brighten as a plan began forming in her mind. It was the turning point. "To hell with them," she announced to me over the phone. And with that she went to the department chairman's office, frightened the poor man almost to death as she demanded to see his copy of the contract, and with great ceremony, tore it up right in front of his unbelieving eyes.

"Dorie, what are you doing?" he squawked.

"Making a political statement," she said as she threw it back over her shoulder.

"But this will mean that THEY will have to start all over again!" he wailed. "All over again!"

She marched to the bus stop all self righteous smiles and straight shoulders. She didn't have the foggiest idea what she was going to do for a job, and she didn't care. Something good would turn up. It always did. And she kept on smiling all the way home just thinking about all the fighting that had already probably begun. "Serves them all right," she told me. "I hope that they drive each other totally nuts." And with that, she began her new resume.

$\mathcal{U}$

The Unitarian Party

Unitarians! The very sound of the word sends horror into my soul. Those awful Unitarians visited us on H Street and almost destroyed the place. It all began when Dorie attended one of their parties with Dave Mindenhall. He was a Unitarian, and very dull, but when he asked her to this party, it was at the end of a boring week, and she had nothing better to do, so she went. She drank too much, and when someone suggested that they have a potluck the following Friday night, she quipped that they could use our house. And they did!

Dorie came into my room the next morning with an awful headache. She plumped yourself down on the edge of the bed, and said, "My God, what are we going to do?"

"Well, it's Saturday morning," I said logically. "I thought that I'd lay here and read a bit."

She looked at me forlornly. "Unitarians are coming!"

"When?"

"Next Friday night."

"How many?"

"Who knows…maybe hundreds!"

"What are they coming here for?"

"A potluck. Hundreds of Unitarians here for a potluck – Oh what on earth are we going to do?"

"Listen, I don't know what you mean by all this WE business," I answered. "I have no intention of staying around to entertain a bunch of strangers! And remember, my room is off-limits!"

"I can't face them alone," she moaned. "Not alone. You've got to help me. Don't desert the ship."

"My god, Dorie, I'm at least as smart as the rats! Of course, I'm leaving the sinking ship. You know that I can't swim!" Dorie left to put the coffee on. We called BS and LC but they and Isiah were going away for the weekend, visiting Isiah's uncle's ranch in Potter Valley.

The only person that wasn't devastated by the idea of the party was Dave, that silly, inane man. "We never plan these things," he told us the next day, "they just come off!" I looked at Dorie and Dorie looked at me. I wanted to choke Dave.

"These things have to be planned," I lectured to Dorie when he left. "You can't just let things happen. What if everybody brings butter and rolls? Huh? And what do they expect for entertainment? And what if someone crashes the party?"

"Well, I can't get out of it. We'll just make a nice wine punch and let the good times roll," she said without conviction.

"There you go with that WE again," I said.

As the time for the party came nearer, we began to plot and plan a great escape. "Let's just up and lock the house and go San Francisco for the weekend," she suggested.

"Or how about calling Dave and telling him that you have the chicken pox," I said.

"We could say that the landlord evicted us and we're in the middle of moving," she said.

"No good," I quipped. "They'd just volunteer to come over and help pack, with our luck."

The afternoon of the party, we moved around the house like ghosts. Neither of us talked. We patted the furniture lovingly like it was the last time we'd see it. An hour before the guests arrived, Dorie got hold of herself and went out to buy the 7 Up and jug wine for the punch. She picked up extra ice cubes at the liquor store, and when she came back, we made about ten gallons of the stuff. "That should do it," she said.

The first guest to arrive was a woman who was twenty minutes early. She was a small, rather timid type, and she carried with her a chocolate cake. "Gee, I'm always early," she whined.

"Put the cake on the table," you said in a friendly enough voice. I put some records on the machine, and poured myself some of the wine punch.

The doorbell rang. The next woman to arrive was big and brassy and she shoved a six-year-old kid ahead of her. "Had to bring Rachel along," she announced. "Couldn't get a sitter. Where can I put this cake?"

"Is it chocolate?" I asked with a smirk on my face.

"Sure is," she replied. "Rachel go over there, sit down, and keep you mouth shut," she instructed the child. The little girl glared back at her mother with evil, little pig eyes.

Next there was a short, fat Greek with a tall, skinny blonde on his arm. When they danced his chin fit between her boobs like a key in a lock. Then there was a gaunt woman in a lavender dress who talked in a high, strange voice as if she was an oracle. She kept asking if George had called yet. The Greek had brought nothing, and the oracle said that George was bringing "her share." After her, came a man who looked and smelled like a ranch hand, a gay couple, a woman who laughed uproariously at everything the ranch hand said, and then they began coming so fast, that it seemed like a whole circus had entered the house.

143

I looked over at the table. There were five chocolate cakes, one coconut cream pie, and one dish of baked chicken legs. That was it. One of the gays was babbling something about baking his own bread, and could we just let him slip it in the oven. It would be done in no time, and had we any butter to go with it?

Dave straggled across the room to me at one point and said, "Isn't this one hell of a party?"

"A real ball," I assured him. I looked over at the punch bowl and saw that it needed refilling. The front door was hanging open for people to come through easily, and the stairs to the upstairs bedroom was thick with people. People smoked and danced, and complained about when the dinner would be served. The smoke was thick, the music was loud, and the lavender woman was crying in one corner because George had stood her up. The phone rang off and on. People called to leave messages for other people. People could be heard to inform the crowd that "Fred had forgotten to bring the salad dressing" and "Where was Alice's condiments," and "The God damned chicken legs were still raw!" The wine punch went down in the bowl like someone was pulling an invisible plug at the bottom. People helped themselves to pots and pans and the refrigerator. The squabbled and bickered, and a fight broke out on the back porch.

I watched the brat, Rachel, slip Dorie's miniature seashell collection into a bag that she had brought in. When I tried to confront her with it, her big-broad mother pulled me aside and told me that I should keep my mouth shut. How could I talk to a little kid that way. I tried to make my way upstairs, and found my bedroom filled with people playing some king of obscene card game. A tall, lanky guy in cut-offs and a T-shirt got stoned in our bathroom, and I found a wilted little grayish woman going through Dorie's closet.

I had to get out of there! The punch was gone, so I was very happy to be elected to make another trip to the liquor store where I tried to stay as long as I could. I was forced back, just in time to hear someone scratch the needle over my favorite record. Someone else yelled, "Hey, I think that that we have a fire here." And the drapes over one window came crashing down. The phone rang, and the lavender woman began to yell horrible, evil things into the receiver. I heard a glass smash, and I knew that I had to leave for good or lose my mind. Price came by about this time, and took one look at me, and said that what I needed was a good, stiff drink at the Pine Cove Inn. Off we went. Dorie looked desperately out the door after us.

About two hours later, my nerves were in better shape, and I suggested to Price that I return. It was about 2:00 a.m. and the bar was closing.

We found Dorie sitting on the front porch smoking. Everything was almost too hushed and quiet. Her dress was stained, her hair straggled around her face, and her feet were bare. I stepped across her and looked into the house.

The floor was covered with chicken bones, discarded plastic forks, and cigarette butts. There were dirty plates everywhere and a viscous goop covered the top of the coffee table. The phone was off the hook. Someone had tossed it into the big wooden salad bowl on the table, and it just laid there with a few wisps of wilted lettuce in the residue of the oil and vinegar dressing. Cushions and record album covers and waded up napkins were tossed on the floor. Someone had ground out a cigar on the surface of Dorie's maple coffee table.

"You should see the kitchen," Dorie said, coming up behind me.

"I can't take it," I whispered.

Price clucked his tongue and said that he really ought to be going.

"Sure," I waved across the living room. "See you later." And we both slumped into chairs. There was complete silence between us.

We sat there about twenty minutes, not knowing what to say, where to begin, or what to do. And then, Dorie rose quite majestically and said, "I've got to get the smell of those people out of this house!" And with that we sprang into action. The mop-up operation was on. We picked up, scrubbed, waxed, repaired, vacuumed, cleaned the upholstery and changed the beds with a furious intensity. We had to eradicate all evidence of those awful Unitarians and their party. About 9:00 a.m., we sat back with great satisfaction. Things were back to normal. We relaxed, talked, shared a pot of hot chocolate and vowed never to invite great, leaping hordes of people in again EVER. And then to treat ourselves for surviving, we got into my car, and drove to the Nut Tree for a wonderful, special lunch! We talked all the way down the freeway about those awful Unitarians.

$\mathcal{V}$

VISIONS

Dorie and I never had plans, per se, but we had visions; otherwise, how would two little farm girls ever have escaped their working class world and early disastrous marriages and gotten master's degrees in literature? We didn't plan our careers as much as we fell into opportunities. So by the end of our year together, Dorie was about to begin a doctoral program, and I was on my way to Iowa to teach at a community college. The prior September when we put our households together, we couldn't have imagined either thing. Our vision included being a member of an academic community and being writers of good fiction. How we were going to achieve this vision? But the one area that eluded our vision was our continued delusional thinking about men. Here for all of our conversations on the subject, we remained bogged down, as the Irish say. Yes, the metaphor of a person trying to make her way slogging through a swamp fit us perfectly. What did we really want, anyway?

I think that was the problem, looking back on our adventures. We just couldn't define our terms. We were too subject to being thrown into a tizzy by any guy that paid attention to us. Today, shrinks would explain this by examining the fact that we wanted to be noticed and held in high esteem by our fathers. But Dorie's mother saw to it that her father was a very distant person, and my parents divorced when I was five, leaving me with an extremely distant father. We just didn't get the good stuff, the bonding that it takes for a little girl to feel loved and appreciated.

If someone had asked us about expectations when it came to men, by the time we lived together, we both would have said, "No lying about marital status." In our little girl world, it never would have occurred to us that married men were on the make. We assumed that once you married, you were honestly committed to your wife and family. Of course, experience should have enlightened us otherwise, but we were too immature to really understand what was happening around us. We bought the mythology, and when it happened to us…men lied to us…we weren't just hurt but outraged. How could they do such a thing? We expected what we generally got from girlfriends. We expected normal social manners such as calling a person if you said you were going to do so. How many times had men said they'd call and never did so. It was a puzzle. Why say it if you weren't going to do it? We expected chivalry. If a man asked you out to dinner, he should pick up the check. Women shouldn't be expected to pay for a date. If you had coffee or a meal with a male friend…I mean a friend, not a date, that was one thing. But a date should pick up the tab. How many times did we sit at a dinner table at the end of a meal when the bill came, only to hear, "Gee, you wanna go dutch?" Or, "Oops, this bill is $10.00 more than I brought tonight. Can you pick up the rest?" And finally, we expected fairness, or what we considered fair. If a guy led you on, and you had a roll in the hay, he should have some level of commitment to you. He should "make an honest woman of you," in our mother's terminology. We didn't want to be sexually exploited, yet we constantly put ourselves in this position.

One little episode in a T.S. Eliot class says it all. Dorie and I sat in a seminar room looking around at the other students, all male. There were about fifteen of them. The professor was extremely boring. I wrote a note to Dorie. "Would you even consider going to bed with any guy in this room?"

"Absolutely not!" she replied.

The ordinary, hard working, socially acceptable guy like Isiah didn't attract us, nor were they attracted to us. We belonged to different worlds. The nice boys with good manners and decent jobs didn't turn us on. No state workers for us. We looked for bad boys, jazzy misfits, men who swaggered and had the devil in their eyes, men who took chances, and did outrageous things. These were the men who broke our hearts. They loved us and left us. Or, they loved us and turned into little boys with no future who needed a momma to take care of them. And then, here came the school marm to the rescue. "He has so much potential," we were heard to say. "If only he would…" Choose your verb to finish that sentence! But even though these types wanted to be taken care of, if you did it for long, they became very resentful, and hated you for it, and you got damn sick and tired of their inability to "be fair" and offer you something. They became another picture in our rogue's gallery.

We often wondered why women with much less going for them…looks, brains, resources… landed handsome, successful men who took care of them. I mean really took care of them financially and emotionally. Even some of the rogues had nice little mousey wives that they adored. Why didn't we get that treatment? "Well, men don't see you two as needing any taking care of," Simon told us. That really made us mad. How did you counter that one?

We could speculate on carousel sex. We could do away with all inhibitions. We could bask in the reward of our careers. We could enjoy each other's company and the company of our gay friends, our girlfriends, but at some deep level we were convinced that we should have a husband in tow, that without a man in our lives, a lawful man, not some random lover, we hadn't really made it as women. That's what our society had taught us, and no matter how we tried, we couldn't really shed that notion. And so our year came to a close, but out conversations about the nature of relationships with men is still going on after fifty years!

WRITERS

By late spring, I had signed a contract to teach English at Fort Dodge Community College in Iowa. Our year together was drawing to a close. I began to make plans to ship my things to my sister's address in Fort Dodge where she would store my boxes in her garage until I arrived in late June. It was about this time that Dorie and I had a discussion that would have a profound effect on both of us. Our question was how were we going to keep up our conversations about men and relationships and relatives, about gossip and intellectual ideas when we would be living 2,000 miles apart. There seemed only one thing to do and that was to write a letter to each other every day. Even a few paragraphs would do. Then at the end of the week, we'd mail the letter. Dorie would save mine and I'd save hers. At the end of the year, we'd ship those letters home. It would keep us in touch, keep the conversation going, and be an on-going record of our lives, a kind of journal. It was a brilliant plan.

As we talked about this plan, we also began to talk about writing in general. We'd written all those academic papers. We taught academic writing, the five paragraph essay, the term paper. We had kept an unofficial journal. When I had run off with Joe, I spent time each day writing to Dorie and she to me. We had included dream analysis, and book analysis, and men analysis in our journals. Dorie began writing poetry. I had put together a few short stories. And then an amazing thing began to happen. "You know what?" Dorie said to me one day. "It's not that we're going to become writers. We already are writers. We may not be any good. We may have a lot to learn. But we haven't studied literature all these years for nothing. I'll bet we could write as well as many of the people we read in magazines, at least."

"Hm," I mouthed. "Let's think about this. Why not try our hand at it. I'll write a story. You edit it, give me your opinion, then I'll rewrite. We could submit our stuff to magazines and publishers. Why not?"

"And I'll do the same," she continued. "If there is anybody whose opinion I would think important, it's you."

"Would you show your work to Simon?" I asked.

She thought about it, lighting a cigarette. She blew smoke into the air. "No," she said finally. "I love Simon, he's my mentor, he gave me my start in college teaching, but on some level, I don't trust him, not with a poem or story. Can't really explain it, but I wouldn't want to share anything with him."

"You know Simon and Evor and the rest of the English professors are supposed to publish or perish. Have you ever seen anything that any of them have written…or anybody in the English Department, except that miserable poet, Ewell?"

"Nothing," she said. "Nothing at all."

A few days later, I dragged out a story from my files. It was about two pookas, Irish mythical creatures that play tricks on people. Fred and Selma were two six foot invisible rabbits who began to visit a woman. Fred wore a green neck tie, and Selma had six brass bracelets on her arm. They began playing tricks on the woman, who eventually began making friends with the pair of them. It was silly and fun and had a good point about friendship. I saw it as a children's book. Why not make a copy for my Children's Literature professor, who was very friendly and nice and interested enough in my teaching career to have written me a nice letter of recommendation. He was a gentle soul. He might even give me some tips on where to send the manuscript to see if I could interest a publisher in it. So, I made a copy, put a top letter with it explaining what I was trying to do with the story, and asked his opinion. And sure enough, a month later, I got a letter in the mail, a fat letter which included my manuscript and his opinion. "This is a waste of your time," he said. "It just doesn't make it as a story. If I were you, I'd throw it out."

I was absolutely crushed beyond words. He had said it wasn't even good enough to be an "F." And the way he said it! Could he have been more cruel? I showed the letter to Dorie who was furious. "That bastard," she yelled. "Why did he have to send you a letter like that? You know what? I think it's a good story, and I'll bet he has never written one in his life! Or, he writes stories but they all get rejected. He's taking it out on you." All I knew was that I felt so ashamed that I'd even put words to paper. My first rejection letter. I should probably get used to it.

In the next few years, I'd write a file cabinet full of stories. So would Dorie. We both had a few successes, essays or stories in local newspapers, but basically we had rejection notices. But something had been born within us that couldn't be corralled ever again, and that was our love of writing. No matter what people at big publishing companies or national magazines had to say, we nursed our grievances, dealt with shame and embarrassment, and kept writing. Novels, stories, poems piled up, and still we kept going.

And the thing that kept us going was our letters because true to our conversations, we wrote those daily letters, and have now done so for fifty years. And what happened as we wrote them? All the practice that every creative writing guru (now making a fortune telling us writers what to do) got done. I found myself writing away about the latest gossip about a colleague, and all of a sudden a character in a story would emerge. I'd work on the setting. I'd write and rewrite the conversations, I'd work on the turn of a phrase, just the right "starting" word. And the magic happened. We got better and better and better.

But the publishing world was changing. Getting an agent was a catch 22 deal. And the years went by. And then via the miracle of technology, we didn't need those New York snobs anymore, those grad students who monitored the slush piles of new writers' submissions. We could do it ourselves. And so we did. Dorie came up with Freshcut Press, and I came up with Pusheen Press. We collaborated with graphic designers, and simple typists, and began putting out our own books. Oh the joy of designing a book all by yourself, of not having to be at the beck and call of some editor that didn't share your vision of the book. (Dorie had certainly gone through that with her PhD thesis, which the University of Oregon wanted to publish but also wanted to rewrite, changing her basic ideas to the point where she hardly recognized her own work. No more of that!)

So fifty years have gone by and we're still writing those letters every day, and we're writing wonderful poems and stories. We're putting out our own stuff and getting really good feedback. And if we could just learn how to market properly (well we know how but don't have the inclination to do it) we might make a break through with the larger reading public yet. It's never been our goal, really. But fantasizing about it is nice. And it all began on H Street and one of our infamous conversations.

$\mathcal{X}$

X-MAS, OR CHRISTMAS

During the 1960s, people began using a short hand term for Christmas. Xmas! We hated it. We were determined to have a real Christmas, getting rid of that modern X. We began the December season by making a list of what we liked and didn't like. We hated holiday parties that turned into drunken brawls. We hated Christmas cards where lurid Santas goosed busty cocktail waitresses. We were determined not to spend the season with most of our relatives. To hell with tradition. And men? We had had enough of men through the years who had done their best to ruin our Christmases. "Out!" we declared. No men would be invited into our home or lives this Christmas. In fact, we would reject anyone, man or woman or child, who would make us cry.

We began the season by decorating the house. We drove my little red Corvair up to Pollock Pines and hunted for a tree, pine cones, small evergreen branches and dried weeds and pieces of bark with moss on them. Laden down with the forest bounty, we drove home and began arranging all these treasures. We decorated the tree with ornaments from the past and new creations made of felt and glitter. We strung a line of twinkling lights on the tree and just about covered it with tinsel. Next, we made wreaths to hang on the front door and in the windows. We set up a manger scene on the coffee table, and suspended real stockings from the bottom window sill. We nestled candles everywhere and put a holiday table cloth on the dining room table. Our home looked so festive.

Now it was time to begin baking. We made cookies and fruit cakes and Dorie's special recipe for cinnamon rolls. We made a big punch bowl of wassail and invited a few lady friends over for the evening. We got our cards written and mailed, and a few packages sent to special relatives and friends. And then it was time to read to each other. I read <u>The Bird's Christmas Carol</u>, and Dorie read Dickens's <u>A Christmas Carol</u>, and we read, taking turns, Truman Capote's <u>A Christmas Memory</u>. And every day when we got up, elves had been at work putting packages all done up in pretty paper and ribbons under the tree, or a new "lump" would appear in our stockings. Both of us had LPs of Christmas music that we took turns putting on the stereo. And we counted down the days until Christmas on an Advent calendar.

We talked about how well this season was going. And we talked about what had gone wrong in the past. We remembered those times when parents were fighting and our Christmas turkey stuck in our throats as we sat around a silent table. We talked of relatives who appeared in our childhoods and made a mess of things. We talked of boyfriends who didn't buy us Christmas presents. We talked of husbands who handed us a checkbook and told us to shop for ourselves. Dorie's husband had knocked over the Christmas tree in a drunken rage one Christmas Eve. My husband bought elaborate gifts for his mother, father, and sister, had filled their house with flower arrangements, and bought expensive champagne for their Christmas breakfast, but had handed me a card (taken from one of the boxes of cards that I was sending out). Inside was a check for $25.00.

I talked about the time when I was eight that I walked on the icy sidewalk in Humboldt, Iowa, slipped and fell and cracked open the head of my new dolly. Dorie talked of the time that her mother knitted her the ugliest gray sweater imaginable. Big, bulky, no style and just plain ugly, while her little sisters got dolls and story books and pretty head scarves. "You are too big for those kind of things," her mother had told her. And after these Christmas reviews, we'd look around at our nest and say our thanks for the new Christmas we were creating, where we didn't have to put up with ugliness or hurt feelings. Simon called to ask if he could come over for the evening. No, we told him. We were busy. Evor called also. "Red flag alert," I mouthed to Dorie as I declined his offer to take me to dinner on Christmas Eve.

Christmas Eve was cold and rain drizzled from the skies as we walked to St. Francis Church late in the evening after having a lovely little repast of homemade vegetable soup and French bread. By the time we got to the church, it was almost filled. We were lucky to get a seat. The only light came from all of the lit candles, and the incense smell was wafting through the air. People tramped inside, shaking off their rain gear and settling into the few pews remaining. There was whiskey on the breath of the old grandpa who sat beside me, a sharp tinny smell of perfume on the woman beside Dorie. Children were dressed in finery, babies were already going to sleep on their mother's laps. A small orchestra began to play soft carols, and then the procession began. Fr. Pat carried the Christchild in his arms and put him in the manger in a life-sized crèche built to one side of the altar. And the mass began. By the time it was over, the rain had stopped and a crisp moon shone overhead as we wended our way home.

The next day, we got up later than usual, had our coffee and cinnamon rolls and opened our presents. Dorie had knitted me a beautiful pink and white afghan. I had purchased her an elegant bejeweled black sweater. Each of us had added things like a book, a fun pair of socks, and a stuffed toy under the tree. I gave Dorie a teddy, and she gave me a stuffed cat. Toys were essential at Christmas, we had both agreed. Next, we watched Bing Crosby's <u>White Christmas</u> on channel 3 of our black and white television. About 3:00, we got all gussied up and went over to our gay friends, Charles and Dave's, for a sumptuous dinner of roast duck, all the trimmings, and French wine. After eating, we sat before their fireplace, looked at the crackling logs and harmonized, singing carols "with the boys," as we called them.

We drove back to H Street, put on flannel nightgowns, had a final cigarette for the evening and contentedly smiled over our season, congratulating ourselves on enjoying the real meaning of friends and religion and symbols of the light hope in the dark season.

"Ah, and what's ahead of us?" we asked.

"Oh my God! New Year's Eve! I exclaimed. "Batten down the hatches!"

"We have to be really careful," Dorie said. Well, Dorie was, but I made the decision to go to a New Year's Eve party with Dr. Price, and you know how that turned out!

Y

YAHOOS

Early one spring morning, I left the house to sit in the coffee shop at 17th and C Streets. It was a place that was good for people watching and practicing writing descriptions. I sat down with a pad of paper on which to make notes and ordered a cup of coffee. An obese woman with rolls and bulges fighting each other for predominance came in arm-in-arm with a cretin of a man. A beautiful brown-eyed three-year-old boy came with them. He was the kind of child that you couldn't bear to think of growing up to look like these two, but already he was a little too chubby in the middle, and his eyes on closer look were a bit vacant. They ordered stacks of pancakes and poured out the contents of a pitcher of maple syrup on them. They sucked up their breakfast and lit cigarettes. The woman coughed until I thought she would retch. They discussed the jukebox selector at their table, and finally played a song about a boy who puts a frog down the dress of his sweetheart. The woman guffawed as she slipped another quarter into the selector. The man put his cigarette out in the remains of his pancakes.

A couple of men walked in wearing hunting jackets. They were woodsy, good-looking men. They ordered coffee, and threw it back as they probably did their whiskey. They began swapping stories about routing lovers out of the backseats of cars, running a hippy off the highway the other day in their jeeps, and one began to talk about the time that the topless dancer agreed to meet him after the show. He twisted his wedding ring around and around his finger as he told the story.

A dark, little man walked in with a colorless shapeless woman beside him. His eyes reminded me of an insect's eyes. He carried a soft lump of a baby that smelled to high heaven of pee. They sat down across from me. They ordered breakfast, and the baby began to cry. The woman was looking at her menu and ignored the cries. The man did the same. A soft new stink of a smell began coming from the baby, and the man looked up from his menu and said, "O God, he shit again." The woman never looked up.

The door opened again and a great bull of a man with a big bushy mustache walked in followed by two identical bulls. The sat at the counter, and the man ordered bacon and eggs for them all. The little bulls looked up at him in adoration. Dishes crashed in the kitchen. The waitress poured more coffee in my cup and asked if that would be all. I nodded and kept taking notes on the people around me.

Four girls strutted into the coffee shop. They had skinny legs sticking out of pre-season cut off jeans. The woodsy men appraised their merits. One of the girls had big pointy breasts which she had just acquired, it seemed, under her T-shirt and she carried them as if they were precious and she so proud of them. The girls ordered cokes, and giggled loudly and keep glancing over at the woodsy men.

A fat young woman slouched in as if she didn't want to be seen. She went to a booth far in the back and I heard her ordering a waffle with whipped cream.

A white Aunt Jemima came in with a shoestring potato of a man. She had shoe-button eyes and a red bandana on her head, and he wore a straw cowboy hat. Her voice was bubbly and happy, and she talked about ordering more oats, and getting the work on the tractor done. She held her cup with both hands, and leaned over it toward the man on the other side of the table. He stretched back against the booth, and listened to her with great attention.

Who were these people and what did they want? Where had they come from this early morning, and where did they call home? Yahoos some would have called them. Just, plain folks. Just common people living near or far from this highway coffee shop. Each with a day ahead of him or her. Each with expectations for that day, and the one that will follow. Each a mystery. Each a joke or a miracle?

Z

ZED

It was Zed, the letter Z in Old English, the final chapter in our alphabet. The end of our year together had come. I was packed and headed to Iowa. Dorie had been accepted at UC Davis in the doctoral program. We decided to spend our last weekend together on the Mendocino Coast in the town of Gualala where Dorie knew of a funky little motel right on the beach. We ate breakfast at a small café sitting Cliffside, and Dorie noticed a "help wanted" sign in the window. She inquired about it. The café needed a waitress, and needed one right away. She applied, and the cook tried her out for the rest of the day. By nightfall, she had landed the job. "Why not spend the summer up here on this beautiful coast, away from the turmoil of Sacramento State, and Sacramento friends. I'd be leaving, and this might be the perfect place to have a new adventure and not sit in the nest that we once shared and feel sad. So, several days later, I drove home alone. Dorie made plans to get a ride to Santa Rosa and take the bus to Sacramento where she would load up her car with everything needed for the summer. Meanwhile she found a room to rent from a friend of the cook.

I planned to drive to Iowa where a moving van had already taken boxes and furniture (my books had been shipped to my sister), check in with the college, find an apartment, and head out for Ireland. Joe had been writing lovesick letters all spring, and I had to have some closure with him. Dorie agreed that I should make the trip, but she was worried about the outcome. So was I. Dorie decided that she had enough in savings to pay the rent on H Street for the summer. She needed a place to come home to in the fall, and then we talked about her coming to spend a week with me at the end of August in Fort Dodge, Iowa, before the school year began after Labor Day.

And so our plans were made. What adventures would befall us before we saw each other again. "Fools rush in where angels fear to tread," we repeated to each other.

"Don't bring that man home again," she instructed me.

"I absolutely promise you that I won't," I declared. And I didn't. But that's another story.

We spent our last evening together at our favorite, Capital Tamale. We toasted each other with champagne cocktails. And over dinner, we discussed the events of our year. Well, we'd never have another garage sale again. And we'd never volunteer a party for a bunch of Unitarians. Philanderers were out. The first question we'd ask a man who asked us out was "are you married?" And then we'd investigate further because everyone knew that men lied. We'd be cautious about dates of any kind, and we'd quickly leave behind energy vampires whether relatives or friends. We were tired of those people that sucked you dry and then leapt over your crumpled body and rushed out to find a new victim. Boundaries! That's what we needed. We laughed at our Rogue's Gallery, and we vowed to not add one more picture on its wall.

And then we talked about writing, our letters, our hopes for our stories, how much time we would spend on writing every day. We talked about plots, stories and characters that we wanted to work on, and we wondered about agents, writing groups, publishers, the business end of writing. There was so much to learn.

We went home that night and sat in the living room, talking, talking, and talking, reluctant to go to bed, to say good night for the last time for the summer. The next morning, we got up early, had our coffee and said our good-byes. We hugged and cried, and I got into the little red Corvair and made my way up the freeway heading for the Sierras on Highway 80. But I wasn't five miles out of town when the feeling of excitement for a new adventure was juxtaposed with a saltiness flavor of sadness in my mouth. I began talking to Dorie about it. I talked to her all the way to Iowa.

I settled in Fort Dodge and began teaching classes: freshman writing, children's literature, and women's studies. I loved the job, but hated the environment. The women colleagues wouldn't take me home to meet their husbands, and the men colleagues weren't about to take me home to meet their wives. It was a lonely existence until I made a special friend named Phillip who also worked in the English Department. We became really good friends, good platonic friends. I wrote to Dorie every day. I sent her copies of stories and poems, and she did the same. We called each other every few weeks even though long distance was still an expensive choice for communication.

In 1973, the Iowa college districts had massive budget problems. After encouraging early retirements, they fired the last hired in each department. That was me. I was ready to leave the scene anyway. I had applied at a little new community college in Ukiah and had secured an interview. So, in May of 1973, I sent my things ahead in a moving van to my mother's address, packed my car, and headed West.

Dorie had never returned to Sacramento the summer that she got that job on the coast. She never entered the PhD program. She met a man, a logger, a gentle bear of a fellow who was definitely not a rogue. And she'd begun writing in earnest. By the fall, she collected her things from H Street and moved to Gualala where she and the bear found a lovely little love nest in a trailer in the woods. She spent her days at her typewriter flushing out novels. She began research on the Mendocino Coast and became acquainted with writing groups, artists, and small shop book sellers in the area. Her essays and stories were being picked up by local newspapers and a few magazines. She had found what she wanted to do and a man to help her do it.

When another friend suggested that I apply for the teaching job in Ukiah, I didn't even know where it was on the map. Squinting at Northern California, I went to B-10, laid my ruler down to follow the line, and there it was – Ukiah – right across the mountain from Gualala. Oh my god! How could this be? Synchronicity with this woman again.

I arrived in Sacramento June 2, checked in at my mother's, and went off to have lunch with BS and LC. BS was pregnant by this time. She and Isiah were having a boy, and she was so excited about the impending birth. True to their plan, they had bought a house in Arden Park, built an apartment onto the back of the house, and moved in LC. LC was very happy that she was going to be an "auntie". She still worked at the dress shop in the Mall, dated men "here and there" as she put it, but she liked her independence. More and more, she said she felt "fulfilled" just as things were; she didn't really need a man in her life except for some fun once in awhile.

I sat there over my shrimp salad, marveling at these two women friends, so different from Dorie and me. So sane, so down-to-earth, so balanced, so happy. Well, it took all kinds to make a world, I thought. I was glad that there were women like BS and LC in the world. But would I have traded places with them for all the energy and chaos in my life? I didn't think so. My adventures had made me the person that I was, the writer that I was, and I wouldn't compromise that for anything.

I made my way to Ukiah, interviewed for the job in the English Department, got a contract, and found an apartment. Dorie was delighted, and so was I. One weekend a month, I drove over the mountain to spend it with herself and Bear (as I came to call him), and the next month, she drove over the mountain in the opposite direction, to spend the weekend with me. Our conversations continued, and during the week, our letters continued to be written too.

After fifty years, I decided to write our story. Well, actually, I gleaned many short stories and start-ups from my files. Both of us had been writing about our experiences for years, fictionalized, of course. I've moved around a lot, teaching at various colleges. In 1980, I returned to Sacramento for good. Dorie actually went to the University of Washington and got her PhD when she was fifty years old. Colleagues and professors told her she'd never get a job at her age. Well, they were wrong! She and Bear moved to Tennessee where she taught at the university for ten years until she retired. Then they returned to their beloved Mendocino County.

And me? Well, as I said, I moved around a lot helping to start English Departments at new community colleges. I had a whirlwind romance with a beautiful Italian, married him, and lived happily ever after... for six years. Then it was time for divorce #2. But I wasn't unhappy about it, and the man and I remained friends. My career has been fulfilling and fun and has kept me going, that and my writing. I'm still at it. And of course, I still begin my daily writes with "Dear Dorie."

And as I think back over all of our adventures, all of the things that we've learned about being women in this world, I smile and think to myself... And it all began on H Street, this steadfast sisterhood, this spiritual connection, this wonderful friendship. And thank God for that!